GROUCHO MARX

★ ★ ★ ★ ★ ★ ★ ★ ★ ★ ★ ★ ★ ★ ★

GROUCHO MARX

★ ★

PETER TYSON

CHELSEA HOUSE PUBLISHERS

New York ★ Philadelphia

CHELSEA HOUSE PUBLISHERS

EDITORIAL DIRECTOR Richard Rennert
EXECUTIVE MANAGING EDITOR Karyn Gullen Browne
COPY CHIEF Robin James
PICTURE EDITOR Adrian G. Allen
ART DIRECTOR Robert Mitchell
MANUFACTURING DIRECTOR Gerald Levine
ASSISTANT ART DIRECTOR Joan Ferrigno

Pop Culture Legends
SENIOR EDITOR Kathy Kuhtz Campbell
SERIES DESIGN Basia Niemczyc

Staff for **GROUCHO MARX**
EDITORIAL ASSISTANT Scott D. Briggs
PICTURE RESEARCHER Wendy P. Wills
COVER ILLUSTRATION Hal Just

First Printing

1 3 5 7 9 8 6 4 2

Library of Congress Cataloging-in-Publication Data

Tyson, Peter.
Groucho Marx / Peter Tyson.
p. cm.—(Pop culture legends)
Includes bibliographical references and index.
ISBN 0-7910-2341-9.
      0-7910-2366-4 (pbk.)
1. Marx, Groucho, 1891–1977—Juvenile literature. 2. Come-
dians—United States—Biography —Juvenile literature. [1. Marx,
Groucho, 1891–1977. 2. Comedians.] I. Title. II. Series.
PN2287.M53T97 1994   94–4797
792.7'028'092—dc20   CIP

FRONTISPIECE:

Groucho Marx is seen here as private detective Wolf J.
Flywheel in M-G-M's *The Big Store,* released in 1941.

Contents ★ ★ ★ ★ ★ ★ ★ ★ ★ ★ ★ ★ ★ ★ ★ ★ ★ ★ ★

A Reflection of Ourselves

Leeza Gibbons

I ENJOY A RARE PERSPECTIVE on the entertainment industry. From my window on popular culture, I can see all that sizzles and excites. I have interviewed legends who have left us, such as Bette Davis and Sammy Davis, Jr., and have brushed shoulders with the names who have caused a commotion with their sheer outrageousness, like Boy George and Madonna. Whether it's by nature or by design, pop icons generate interest, and I think they are a mirror of who we are at any given time.

Who are *your* heroes and heroines, the people you most admire? Outside of your own family and friends, to whom do you look for inspiration and guidance, as examples of the type of person you would like to be as an adult? How do we decide who will be the most popular and influential members of our society?

You may be surprised by your answers. According to recent polls, you will probably respond much differently than your parents or grandparents did to the same questions at the same age. Increasingly, world leaders such as Winston Churchill, John F. Kennedy, Franklin D. Roosevelt, and evangelist Billy Graham have been replaced by entertainers, athletes, and popular artists as the individuals whom young people most respect and admire. In surveys taken during each of the past 15 years, for example, General Norman Schwarzkopf was the only world leader chosen as the number-one hero among high school students. Other names on the elite list joined by General Schwarzkopf included Paula Abdul, Michael Jackson, Michael Jordan, Eddie Murphy, Burt Reynolds, and Sylvester Stallone.

More than 30 years have passed since Canadian sociologist Marshall McLuhan first taught us the huge impact that the electronic media have had on how we think, learn, and understand—as well as how we choose our heroes. In the 1960s, Pop artist Andy Warhol predicted that there would soon come a time when every American would be famous for 15 minutes. But if it is easier today to achieve Warhol's 15 minutes of fame, it is also much harder to hold on to it. Reputations are often ruined as quickly as they are made.

And yet, there remain those artists and performers who continue to inspire and instruct us in spite of changes in world events, media technology, or popular tastes. Even in a society as fickle and fast moving as our own, there are still those performers whose work and reputation endure, pop culture legends who inspire an almost religious devotion from their fans.

Why do the works and personalities of some artists continue to fascinate us while others are so quickly forgotten? What, if any, qualities do they share that enable them to have such power over our lives? There are no easy answers to these questions. The artists and entertainers profiled in this series often have little more in common than the enormous influence that each of them has had on our lives.

Some offer us an escape. Artists such as actress Marilyn Monroe, comedian Groucho Marx, and writer Stephen King have used glamour, humor, or fantasy to help us escape from our everyday lives. Others present us with images that are all too recognizable. The uncompromising realism of actor and director Charlie Chaplin and folk singer Bob Dylan challenges us to confront and change the things in our world that most disturb us.

Some offer us friendly, reassuring experiences. The work of animator Walt Disney and late-night talk show host Johnny Carson, for example, provides us with a sense of security and continuity in a changing world. Others shake us up. The best work of composer John Lennon and actor James Dean will always inspire their fans to question and reevaluate the world in which they live.

It is also hard to predict the kind of life that a pop culture legend will lead, or how he or she will react to fame. Popular singers Michael Jackson

and Prince carefully guard their personal lives from public view. Other performers, such as popular singer Madonna, enjoy putting their private lives before the public eye.

What these artists and entertainers do share, however, is the rare ability to capture and hold the public's imagination in a world dominated by mass media and disposable celebrity. In spite of their differences, each of them has somehow managed to achieve legendary status in a popular culture that values novelty and change.

The books in this series examine the lives and careers of these and other pop culture legends, and the society that places such great value on their work. Each book considers the extraordinary talent, the stubborn commitment, and the great personal sacrifice required to create work of enduring quality and influence in today's world.

As you read these books, ask yourself the following questions: How are the careers of these individuals shaped by their society? What role do they play in shaping the world? And what is it that so captivates us about their lives, their work, or the images they present?

Hopefully, by studying the lives and achievements of these pop culture legends, we will learn more about ourselves.

A Night on Broadway

O N THE NIGHT OF MAY 19, 1924, Groucho Marx's mother, Minnie Marx, was carried down the center aisle of New York's Casino Theatre on a stretcher. Earlier that day, while being fitted for a new dress, she had fallen off a chair and fractured a leg. Waving and smiling to a cheering audience, she settled into a front row box seat.

"I doubt if anyone ever entered a theater more triumphantly than she did," recalled Groucho, the leader of the comedy team known as the Marx Brothers, in his book *Groucho and Me*. Mrs. Marx's sons were about to open their own show on Broadway, and, said Groucho, "a little thing like a broken leg was not going to rob her of that supreme moment."

That night was even more momentous for Groucho and his brothers. For as they prepared to take the stage, they knew their performance that evening could make or break their careers.

The Marx Brothers had become big stars in vaudeville, a live stage show consisting of a series of short, usually comic acts. The menu at a vaudeville show commonly comprised a smorgasbord of dialogue, pantomime, singing,

The Marx Brothers (from left to right, Harpo, Chico, Zeppo, and Groucho) appear with Carlotta Miles (as Empress Joséphine) in the Napoléon scene from the 1924 musical comedy revue *I'll Say She Is*.

dancing, and sometimes acrobatics, juggling, and animal performances—a kind of circus of the stage. Before movies, radio, and television swept it away, vaudeville offered the public a cheap form of entertainment, costing as little as 10 cents a show. Beginning with the Four Nightingales, which Minnie Marx had formed in 1907 when Groucho was 16 years old, the brothers had crisscrossed the country on the vaudeville circuits. By the start of World War I, they had become big-time vaudeville stars, performing at the nation's top venues, including New York's Palace Theatre, run by the leading vaudeville producer of the day, E. F. Albee.

Vaudeville was looked down upon by some as the slums of entertainment. For vaudevillians, as for all stage performers, the real stamp of approval came from being well received on Broadway, the heart of America's theatrical world. Thus, Groucho and his brothers Chico, Harpo, and Zeppo knew that opening night of their new show, *I'll Say She Is,* would be the most consequential of their professional lives.

Two years before, the Marx Brothers had hit an all-time low. In 1922, they had taken their act to London's Coliseum Theatre. In those days, an English audience showed its displeasure with an act by tossing pennies onto the stage. When this happened at the Coliseum, Groucho leaned out into the audience and said, "We've come a long way to entertain you. The least you could do is throw silver." That ad-lib, a harbinger of the spontaneous comic style that would soon make him world famous, got one of the evening's few laughs. The show flopped, making "no sensation at all," as one reviewer put it, and forcing the Marx Brothers to revert to older material for the rest of their three-week stay.

Back in the States, their careers took another blow. Apparently E. F. Albee, their producer, had grown furious that the brothers had played in London without his permission. Distrustful of authority even when it was on their side, the brothers did nothing to placate Albee. In fact, they antagonized him further by signing with New York's other major vaudeville circuit, Shubert Brothers. But Shubert Brothers soon went under, taking its new clients with it. Even more enraged that they had snubbed him, Albee ensured that the Marx Brothers, despite their established name, gained no work, even in the small-time vaudeville houses in "the provinces," as New Yorkers tended to label any place beyond the hallowed precinct of Broadway. Having reached the summit of vaudeville, the Marx Brothers almost vanished altogether.

Then one day Chico met a producer who was eager to put to use some costly scenery from an earlier show of his that had failed, and he offered to finance a Marx Brothers act. Groucho and his brothers jumped at the opportunity. Within three weeks, they put together a show. The title came from a popular exchange of the day: "Isn't she a beauty?" "I'll say she is!" Like all of their vaudeville shows, *I'll Say She Is* borrowed material from their previous acts—time-tested comedy scenes that were all but guaranteed to bring laughs. The show opened at the Walnut Street Theatre in Philadelphia, Pennsylvania, and became an immediate hit, playing 17 weeks at capacity and touring "the provinces" for a year.

The Marxes then had to make a choice. Should they continue trying to book the show in small-time vaudeville houses, or should they take it to Broadway, risking lambasting by the merciless New York critics?

Groucho, who earned his nickname for being grouchy and pessimistic, was not convinced the Marx Broth-

Minnie Marx, mother of the Marx Brothers, was carried down the center aisle of New York's Casino Theatre on the opening night of her sons' Broadway show. Years earlier Mrs. Marx had managed her boys' vaudeville act, then called the Four Nightingales, and toured across the country with them.

ers had the talent to make it on Broadway. Besides, putting on a Broadway show in those days took as much as $200,000. Chico, however, urged his brothers to give it a try, and they received just enough funds from their backer to make it happen. To save money, they gathered additional stage scenery themselves. "We cut enough corners," Groucho later quipped, "to build a whole new street."

As the marquee lights went on at the Casino Theatre on May 19, Groucho grew tense. At the time, there were just five or six critics in New York whose words could start—or finish—an entertainer's career. Just before he took the stage, Groucho learned that, because of the last-minute cancellation of another show, the city's leading commentators were in the audience that night. So, not far from a beaming Minnie Marx sat the foremost theater pundits of the day, glowering because they had to critique this little-known, surely second-rate act.

I'll Say She Is was billed as a musical comedy revue, though really it was a vaudeville show with a classier name. Featuring 24 individual skits, it follows the fortunes of a rich, spoiled young woman who will marry the man who gives her the biggest thrill. During the course of the show, the Marx Brothers, assuming different roles, court the woman (played by Carlotta Miles) in a Chinatown opium den, a Wall Street boardroom, and the mansion of a wealthy man who drapes her in exotic clothes from around the world.

In the show's finale, Groucho portrays the French emperor Napoléon I, who bids a prolonged farewell to his wife, Joséphine, as he heads off to war. For the scene, Groucho donned a French general's uniform, with high black boots, a sword, and a three-cornered hat. (He also wore wire-rimmed spectacles with no lenses and absurdly thick, painted-on black eyebrows and mustache—his trademarks.) Every time Groucho, as Napoléon, leaves

the stage to meet his troops, Chico, Harpo, and Zeppo
(playing, respectively, François, Gaston, and Alphonse,
Napoléon's trusted advisers) appear individually from
beneath couches and behind curtains to woo Joséphine.
Again and again, Napoléon returns to fetch his sword,
which he claims he has forgotten, but, despite his suspi-
cions, he always finds Empress Joséphine alone:

> *Empress:* Oh! It's you. I thought you were at the front.
> *Napoléon:* I was, but nobody answered the bell, so I came
> around here.
> *Empress:* Well, what are you looking for?
> *Napoléon:* My sword—I lost my sword.
> *Empress:* There it is, dear, just where you left it.
> *Napoléon:* How stupid of you. Why didn't you tell me?
> Look at that point. I wish you wouldn't open sardines with
> my sword. I am beginning to smell like a delicatessen. My
> infantry is beginning to smell like the cavalry.

These lines from the scene, which Groucho cowrote with
cartoonist Will B. Johnstone, exemplify the kind of
humor that Groucho brandished like Napoléon's sword
for more than 60 years in show business. In this excerpt
from the original script, which Groucho found in a desk
drawer years later, distinguishing features of his unique
style stand out: the simplest of plots, serving as nothing
more than a shaky platform for his verbal antics; a kind
of comic double-talk that has Groucho making light of
the weightiest themes (in this case, war, infidelity, love);
an unabashed use of double entendre, in which he forever
catches the listener off guard by using another meaning
of a word or phrase than the one expected (for example,
the front of the house instead of the war front); the silliest
comedy (which has the great French emperor chastising
his wife for opening cans of fish with his prized sword);
and insults ("How stupid of you"), which became
Groucho's stock-in-trade. Coupled with a flawless delivery and visual cues, such as his soon-to-be-famous leer

and a roll of his bulbous brown eyes, Groucho's act often left audiences in tears of laughter.

Thus, although the show the Marx Brothers put on that night might have been staged on a shoestring, it offered superior comic talent. As Groucho recalled, "The scenery didn't quite fit, and the score was probably the most undistinguished one that ever bruised the eardrums of a Broadway audience. . . . What we did have, however, was something money couldn't buy. We had 15

Zeppo, Harpo, Groucho, and Chico Marx pose for a photograph at the Palace Theatre in New York. Groucho was not convinced that the Marx Brothers had the talent to make it on Broadway; but the morning after *I'll Say She Is* opened, the show received the critics' raves.

years of sure-fire comedy material, tried-and-true scenes that had been certified by vaudeville audiences from coast to coast."

Such zany, nonsensical comedy did not typify musical revues of the day, which featured a more structured plot and more sophisticated song-and-dance numbers. Groucho had no idea how the jaded New York critics would respond, so it was with some trepidation that he slipped out the next morning to get the newspapers and read the reviews of the show.

What he read changed his life. As he later quipped, "The critics swooned with joy. And when they came to, they raved ecstatically." The *New York Post*'s critic wrote, "The Marx Brothers have left your correspondent too limp with laughter to do more than gasp incoherently at the most." Fay King wrote in the *Daily Mirror,* "There are 'easy marks,' German marks, dollar marks and laundry marks, but on Broadway, when you mention Marx, you mean the four merry young men who instill so much real comedy and hilarious humor in that exceptionally colorful and charming musical show at the Casino Theatre." For Groucho, the ultimate accolade came from Charlie Chaplin, the top comedian of the day, who hailed *I'll Say She Is* as "the best musical comedy revue I've ever seen."

Almost two decades after he joined his first vaudeville act, Groucho had become, literally overnight, a Broadway star. The Marx Brothers' outlandish comedy perfectly suited the jovial, free-spirited mood of the country in the mid-1920s. Having finally put the aching memory of the Great War behind them, Americans were going, as the writer F. Scott Fitzgerald put it, "on the greatest, gaudiest spree in history." At long last, the nation was ready for the Marx Brothers.

2 Growing Up Fast

GROUCHO WAS BORN Julius Henry Marx on October 2, 1890. His parents were poor Jewish immigrants who lived on East Ninety-third Street in the Yorkville section of New York City. Though Julius would someday be wealthy, in the early years of his life poverty dictated how he lived and thought. He might never have entered show business had the family not needed the money, and poverty shaped the characters the Marx Brothers later portrayed: penniless, down-and-out men, who, though of decent moral character, always sought to scrounge a buck.

Julius came by his trade honestly. In the late 1800s his maternal grandparents, the Schoenbergs, traveled throughout Germany with their 11 children—including Julius's mother, Minnie—in a theater wagon, putting on shows wherever they could find an audience. Julius's grandfather, Lafe "Opie" Schoenberg, juggled, while his grandmother, Fannie "Omie" Schoenberg, played the harp. Soon after the Schoenbergs immigrated to the United States in the early 1880s, Minnie met an immigrant named Simon

---

Julius (top, center) and Leonard (second from right) appear in a photograph with two friends, circa 1894. Friend Bernie Smith once said of Julius, "He was never a big strong boy. He was always kind of frail. . . . The only protection he had was his wit."

Marx, who had recently arrived from Alsace-Lorraine in France. Minnie and Simon married in 1884.

To earn a living, Simon became a tailor. Frenchie, as everyone knew him, had no training in tailoring and, as it turned out, no talent either, so the Marxes lived on the edge of indigence throughout Julius's childhood. ("Look at me," Julius said years later in the film *Monkey Business,* "I worked my way up from nothing to a state of extreme poverty.") Not until Julius and his brothers began bringing home earnings as teenage performers did money enter the Marx household in any significant amount. But the children never went hungry: where Frenchie failed with cloth he succeeded brilliantly with food, "making ambrosia out of potato peels," wrote biographer Hector Arce in *The GrouchoPhile.*

Minnie, meanwhile, spent her time raising children. She bore six, though as Groucho later recalled in characteristically droll style, "the oldest, Manfred, died of old age. He was three at the time." The other five were: Leonard, born on March 26, 1887; Adolph, born on November 21, 1888; Julius Henry, born on October 2, 1890; Milton, born in (there is some uncertainty about Milton's exact date of birth) 1897; and Herbert, born on February 25, 1901. They were later to become, respectively, Chico, Harpo, Groucho, Gummo, and Zeppo, but for now, they were just five more anonymous children living in tenements on New York's Upper East Side. Then as now, to get by on the tough inner-city streets, one had to grow up fast and learn to look out for oneself.

"He was never a big strong boy. He was always kind of frail," the producer Bernie Smith said of Julius in *The Secret Word Is Groucho.* "In a fight he didn't have a prayer. The only protection he had was his wit. He would get a friend or foe off balance by saying something."

Julius's quick mind made up for his lack of formal education. Like many children of poor, working parents,

the Marx boys had to quit school to work, including Julius at age 14. As he put it laconically, "I had to leave school in the seventh grade—nobody, after all, should stay in school after the age of 22—but I would regard Yale as my alma mater." Although he makes light of it here, Julius's curtailed education plagued him throughout his life. In time he became not only one of the century's greatest comedians but also a widely read author, yet he never overcame the inadequacy he felt around well-educated people.

Julius needed little schooling, however, to handle his first job. For $3.50 a week, he answered the telephone in a one-person real estate office. At first he was conscientious, but the phone never rang, and every day his employer arrived later and left earlier, until he rarely came in at all. Without calls, Julius's services were hardly needed, so he, too, began slimming his hours. One day, while playing hooky at the ballpark, he retrieved a hat

Hannah Schickler, Lou Levy, and Julius, Milton, Minnie, and Adolph Marx are seen here as the Six Mascots. Groucho is leading the act in the song "Das ist nicht ein Schnitzelbank" (That is not a sawbuck [a 10-dollar bill]).

21

that had blown off a man's head. The man turned out to be his boss, and Julius was promptly fired.

His next job landed him in his life's chosen field. At age 15, he read a classified ad in the *New York Morning World:* boy singer sought for vaudeville act, room and board and four dollars per week. He ran all the way to the audition. There he found a middle-aged man dressed in a kimono and wearing lipstick—a female impersonator. "This was the profession I wanted to get into?" he later asked rhetorically. After hearing Julius, who had sung soprano in his school choir, the man turned to the other boys waiting for their chance and yelled, "Get out!"

The man's name was Robin Larong, and Julius had just become the third member of the Larong Trio. "I felt that for the first time in my life I wasn't a nonentity," he later wrote. For the act, he and another boy wore bellboy suits and matching pillbox hats. Their first engagement was in Grand Rapids, Michigan, followed by a split week in Cripple Creek and Victor, Colorado. In vaudeville, wherever one could book engagements, there one played, whether it was down the street or across the country.

What happened on that journey—and on one that was to follow soon after—fed Julius's lifelong distrust of authority. For after playing in Colorado, Larong ran off with the act's other member, taking Julius's two-week salary of eight dollars with him and leaving Julius penniless. To earn enough money to get home, the future Groucho Marx drove a horse-drawn grocery wagon between the two mountain towns in which he had so recently performed.

Back in New York, Julius signed onto another act, little suspecting that history has a way of repeating itself. He joined a dramatic troupe for an eight-week tour from Norfolk, Virginia, to New Orleans, Louisiana. Playing the coachman in an act called *The Coachman and the*

Lady, Julius dressed in a purple jacket with brass buttons, white trousers tucked into purple boots, and a yellow silk hat. The tour went well, but after its last performance in New Orleans, the Englishwoman who ran the act (and played the Lady) put him on a New York–bound train with a small bag that supposedly contained his payment of $65. It did not. The Lady had run off with a married lion tamer from another act and had taken Julius's money with her. "I determined then and there," Groucho held later, "that the next elopement I financed would be my own."

Minnie, too, abhorred such treatment and decided to take her son's fledgling career into her own hands. In 1907 she formed the Three Nightingales, composed of Julius, his brother Milton, and a young friend, Mabel O'Donnell. Soon Julius's brother Adolph replaced O'Donnell, and a fourth member named Lou Levy joined the act, which became the Four Nightingales. Minnie outfitted them in sailor suits with white straw hats, clip-on bow ties, and paper lapel roses and taught them various song-and-dance numbers. Under her shrewd leadership, which included moving the family to Chicago in 1910 to be more central to the national vaudeville circuits, the Four Nightingales became a huge success. For four years the quartet toured the country, performing as many as 30 shows a week and earning as much as $200 a week.

For the Marxes, such earnings represented riches, yet Minnie strove to conserve every penny as they traveled to distant cities to perform. "Because we were a kid act, we traveled at half-fare, despite the fact that we were all around 20," Groucho reminisced years later. "Minnie insisted we were 13. 'That kid of yours is in the dining car smoking a cigar,' the conductor told her. 'And another one is in the washroom shaving.' Minnie shook her head sadly. 'They grow so fast.'"

On occasion, Minnie's talents as a manager made her overambitious. Because salaries for small-time vaudeville acts were often based on the number of performers in the show, Minnie decided one day to add herself and her sister Hannah to the act, which was promptly renamed the Six Mascots. "The fact that neither my mother nor her sister had the slightest talent didn't bother my mother in the least," Groucho wrote. "She said she knew many people in show business who didn't have any talent. At the moment she was looking at me."

Minnie was then 50 years old, her sister 55, yet Minnie determined they should portray a pair of guitar-playing schoolgirls. The improbability of their act played itself out onstage. During one of the Six Mascots' first gigs, the sisters, who had removed their glasses to look younger, accidentally sat on the same chair. The chair collapsed, dropping them indecorously to the floor. Wisely, Minnie decided performing was not her forte and changed the act back to the Four Nightingales.

Around 1910, Lou Levy quit, and the act became the Marx Brothers and Company.

Fittingly, it was during this incarnation that Julius found his calling. It occurred one night in the small Texas town of Nacogdoches. The brothers were performing in a circus tent before a crowd of "big ranchers in ten-gallon hats and smaller ranchers in five-gallon hats," Groucho later joked. Suddenly the crowd, almost to a person, stood up and strode out of the tent.

By the time the townspeople sauntered back in, a half hour later, Julius and his cohorts were spitting mad. The Marx Brothers had been working harder than they ever had, and they were exhausted. How dare these people treat our efforts so casually, Julius thought. (Unbeknownst to him, the ranchers had only left to help lasso a runaway mule.) To vent his rage, Julius began making a shambles of their carefully prepared act. "This quickly

The Marx Brothers—Milton (top left), Adolph (top right), and Julius (seated at center)—are photographed with the cast of *Fun in Hi Skule*. Julius played the German teacher Mr. Green, a polished wisecracker, who became the foundation of all future characters written for him.

evolved into a rough-house comedy bit, with the Marxes, led by Groucho, flinging insults about Texas and its inhabitants to the audience as rapidly as they could think of them," wrote Groucho's son Arthur 30 years later in *My Life with Groucho*. No longer caring what the audience thought, Julius worked lines like "Nacogdoches is full of roaches" into his standard songs, fully expecting, reported Arthur, "to be tarred and feathered and run out of town on a rail."

To Julius's surprise, the audience reveled in the assault, laughing hardest at the lines meant to infuriate them. Just when the brothers had reached their wits' end, the pressure suddenly eased. Those few hours in a circus tent out on the Texas plains represented a watershed. For the act, it marked the beginning of the transition to comedy. For Julius, it revealed in a stroke his innate ability to fashion jokes on the spot and to make people laugh even as he cut them down to size. In time, Julius learned to ad-lib and to insult better than anyone else alive, and it is for these talents that Groucho Marx is best remembered.

When word of the Marx Brothers' boisterous performance reached the nearby town of Denison, Texas, the manager of the local theater offered to book them—and raise their weekly salary from $50 to $75—if they promised to add a comedy sketch to their normal act. Adolph and Milton balked at the idea of producing a comic bit on such short notice, but Julius, sensing that he and his brothers had a chance to become something more than just another child singing act, took pen to paper and wrote a new skit. Because Denison was about to host a teachers' convention, Julius crafted a schoolroom routine that combined remembrances from his own short-lived school days with ideas borrowed from other school acts that were popular at the time. Called *Fun in Hi Skule,* the act concerned an unruly class led ineffectually by a German teacher named Mr. Green (played by Julius).

Like the night in Nacogdoches, *Fun in Hi Skule* signified an advance on several levels for Julius. First, it revealed Julius as the leader and driving force behind the Marx Brothers. Second, it

Julius, seen here when he first entered entertainment at age 15, emerged as the leader of the Marx Brothers during the tour of *Fun in Hi Skule.* The skit proved that Julius could write and make people laugh.

proved to him that he could write, and it launched what later became a lucrative writing career, which he later maintained made him more proud than any of his acting roles. Third, with *Fun in Hi Skule* Julius learned to use satire and other comic tools to assuage the guilt he felt in not having finished high school—a technique he used both professionally and personally all his life. Finally, Julius realized he could make people laugh. With the new act, Julius and the Marx Brothers became comedians. Subtitled "An Artistic Screamingly Funny Howling Masterpiece," *Fun in Hi Skule* featured pure comic sketches, and its songs bore more of the burgeoning Marx Brothers' nutty stamp. For example, the first verse of "Peasie Weasie," one of the act's songs, ran like this:

My mother called Sister downstairs the other day.
"I'm taking a bath," my sister did say.
"Well, slip on something quick, here comes Mr. Brown."
She slipped on the top step and then came down.

Singing and dancing would always play a part in Marx Brothers efforts, on stage and screen, but from now on they would take a back seat to comedy. In this and other ways, *Fun in Hi Skule* laid the groundwork for all coming Marx Brothers endeavors. Adolph, about to become Harpo, donned his soon-to-be-famous curly-haired wig and further honed his Irish bumpkin character, Patsy Brannigan. Leonard, the future Chico, joined the act for the first time as straight man to Julius. Julius's character, the erudite wisecracker Mr. Green, formed the foundation of all future characters written for Julius, whether for the stage, radio, or film.

Fun in Hi Skule had audiences roaring in Denison and around the country, which it toured from 1910 to 1913 (and in an abridged form called *Mr. Green's Reception,* for two additional years). In more than just name, Julius was about to become Groucho.

3 ★ Hitting the Big Time

ONE NIGHT IN 1914, in the middle of a week-long performance in Galesburg, Illinois, Julius assumed his new name. "We were sitting around backstage playing poker with a monologuist named Art Fisher," Groucho recalled, "and talk got around to how *Sherlocko, the Monk,* a popular comic strip of the time, had infected vaudeville with all sorts of Henpeckos and Tightwados and Nervos."

Fisher took his cue. Unwittingly making history at that moment, he bestowed on each of his new friends, the Marxes, a Sherlocko-inspired nickname. He called Milton "Gummo" because he wore gumshoes. Adolph the harpist became "Harpo." When he was not gambling, Leonard chased women, so Fisher dubbed him "Chicko" (a typesetting error later made it Chico). Finally, the grumpy Julius became "Groucho." (No one knows for certain how Herbert, the youngest brother and not yet a part of the act, gained his stage name "Zeppo.")

The show the brothers had presented that night in Illinois was *Home Again,* a vaudeville act they developed in 1914 and used for five years. One of

Gummo (Milton), Groucho (Julius), and Harpo (Adolph) pose with Uncle Julius (center), whom they called the General. The Marx Brothers received their nicknames, which were inspired by the comic strip *Sherlocko, the Monk,* during a poker game in Galesburg, Illinois, in 1914.

Groucho's uncles, Minnie's brother Al Shean, a successful vaudevillian, took it upon himself to write a new script for his nephews, who had grown tired of *Mr. Green's Reception. Home Again* was ostensibly about a rich American named Henry Jones (played by Groucho), who is returning from a trip to Europe with his wife and two children. The act opens on the Cunard cruise ship dock in New York City, "an illusion conveyed," wrote the critic S. J. Perelman, "by four battered satchels and a sleazy backdrop purportedly representing the gangway of the *Brittanic.*"

Groucho established the play's tone with his first line, delivered as he steps off the ship's gangway: "Well, friends, next time I cross the ocean I'll take a train. I'm certainly glad to set my feet on terra firma. Now I know that when I eat something I won't see it again." As in all Marx Brothers efforts, the plot was, noted Perelman, "sheerest gossamer." Groucho and his brothers used plot like a launching pad: once in the air, they were on their own, with Groucho ad-libbing and Chico playing along and Harpo inventing new mime antics on the spot. *Home Again* was no exception. When the gags ran out at the gangway at the end of act 1, Henry Jones invited everyone to a party at his villa beside the Hudson River in upstate New York (act 2). There the risible dialogue continued. For instance, Henry Jones's son Harold (played by Gummo) tells his father, "Patsy Brannigan the garbage man is here," to which Groucho responds, "Tell him we don't want any."

Home Again further molded the basic characters that the Marx Brothers would assume throughout their careers. Drawing on previous successes, Harpo once again portrayed the yokel Patsy Brannigan with his moplike wig. When Shean realized, upon finishing the *Home Again* script, that he had given the naturally reticent Harpo only three lines, he cut the lines and explained that from that moment on, Harpo would pantomime. Harpo never spoke again on-stage or in the movies, and he became argu-ably the greatest mime of his day. In *Home Again,* Harpo also performed a harp solo, and Chico a piano solo, as they would in all future Marx Brothers undertakings.

Shean gave Chico the character Tony Saroni, because some said the eldest Marx brother, with his dark eyes and hair, looked Italian. For the rest of his career, Chico impersonated an "Eye-talian," with his modified Tyrolean outfit and simulated Italian accent. Shean also wrote him in as Harpo's "interpreter" as well as the principal straight man to Groucho, and in this capac-ity he served throughout his life. "I'd like-a to say goombye to your wife," Tony Saroni says on the gangway to Mr. Jones, who replies, "Who wouldn't?"

Such shameless impertinence defined Groucho's character. Whether he was Henry Jones the traveler, or Captain Jeffrey T. Spaulding the African explorer (from the Broadway show and film *Animal Crackers*), or Otis B. Driftwood (from the film *A Night at the Opera*), Groucho was really just Groucho the cheeky comedian. Like the plot, his fictional personality served only as a mental mannequin on which to hang whatever comic dressing suited Groucho at the time. From this point on, Groucho's characters also had at their disposal a host of trademark props, including—besides the greasepaint and glasses—a long frock coat, mussed-up hair parted in the middle, and a cigar. "It gave you time to think," Groucho once said of his ever present stogie. "You could tell a joke, and if the audience didn't laugh, you could take some

Minnie Marx's brother Alfred Schoenberg, known as Al Shean, had become popular in a vaudeville act with Ed Gallagher. In 1914, Shean penned *Home Again,* in which Harpo began his career as a mime. Shean wrote Chico in as Harpo's interpreter and as chief straight man to Groucho's zany character named Henry Jones.

31

puffs on the cigar." By this time he could also fall back on his "duck walk," a ludicrous, crouching stride that got him to his destination in half the steps of a normal walk—and had audiences rolling on the floor.

With *Home Again,* Groucho became the undisputed leader of the Marx Brothers. The team's chief actor and comedian, he was also its manager. Though older than Groucho, Chico and Harpo preferred to spend their free time on gambling and women. Groucho drank little, refused to gamble, and rarely pursued women (despite his onstage brazenness, he suffered from acute shyness around women). Conscientious to a fault, Groucho worried constantly—about money, about their next act, and about whether they were funny enough or, worst of all fates, "washed up." Arthur Marx once commented that his father's "almost pathological" concern for the future played a key role in Groucho's long-lived popularity, for it "never allowed him to become complacent about his career or to take his ability for granted."

Home Again toured the country from 1914 to 1919. During the production's first years, the Marx Brothers worked as hard as they ever had, traveling from city to city, typically playing four shows a day Monday through Friday and five a day on weekends, for a total of 30 appearances a week. "Why, outside the necessity of sheer survival, did we do this?" Groucho asked rhetorically. "We all wanted to be the best, the most perfect, the most flawless, the funniest that we could possibly be. Nobody else could be funny for you."

Their efforts paid off. By the end of World War I, they had hit the big time, playing only two shows a day and earning the then very respectable sum of $1,500 per week. The Marx Brothers appeared so often at New York's Palace Theatre, the country's choicest vaudeville house, that they became known as "Palace regulars." They went on to hold the record among big-time acts for having played 60 consecutive weeks in the city's first-class vaude-ville theaters.

Home Again and other theatrical farces had worked like a salve on the uneasiness many Americans felt in the years leading up to the war. The exuberant confidence felt during President Theodore Roosevelt's tenure (1901–9) had given way, by 1913, to the uncertain prewar years presided over by the introspective President Woodrow Wilson. Americans craved humor, especially after the nation entered the war in 1917. Broadway, which had just begun its rise to preeminence with stars like Fanny Brice and Will Rogers, was the place to find it. After the Treaty of Versailles ended World War I in 1919, *Home Again* struck an especially personal chord with citizens welcoming home their hard-fighting doughboys from Europe.

The decade was a time of experimentation for artists of all kinds. Pablo Picasso and Georges Braque invented a radically new form of art called cubism, poets Ezra Pound and Amy Lowell wrote free verse and founded Imagism, and actresses such as Mary Pickford and Pearl White heralded the age of the movie queen. Never one to miss a trend, Groucho, too, experimented, both in and outside of show business. Around 1913, he and his brothers created a one-hour musical show called *Cinderella Girl.* Subtitled "A Merry Melange of Mirth, Melody, and Music," the show was the Marx Brothers' first and only attempt at a legitimate musical show. *Cinderella Girl* was a flop, but it introduced Chico's piano-playing skills for the first time and encouraged Harpo to take up the harp. By bringing Chico into the act full-time, it also further solidified the Marx Brothers comedy team. The final adjustment came in 1918, when Zeppo replaced Gummo, who joined the army. (Gummo never returned to the act and later became a theatrical agent.)

Zeppo (kneeling), the youngest Marx, replaced Gummo in 1918 and played the romantic roles in the Marx Brothers act. Harpo's harp playing and Chico's piano playing had already become regular parts of the Marx Brothers routine.

While the war raged, the four brothers bought a farm in La Grange, Illinois, about 20 miles outside Chicago, ostensibly to raise vegetables and chickens to aid the war effort. It soon became clear that the Marx Brothers were as suited to farming as they were to musicals, as Groucho later explained—placing facts, as usual, rather freely at the disposal of humor: "The first morning on the farm, we got up at five. The following morning, we dawdled in bed until six. By the end of the week we were getting up at noon, which was just enough time for us to get dressed to catch the 1:07 to Wrigley Field, where the Chicago Cubs played." Although the farm failed and the Marxes soon sold it, the experience planted the seed of Groucho's later passion for gardening.

Another failed effort that presaged things to come was *Humor Risk,* a silent film that each brother put up $1,000 to produce around 1920. "We made two reels that didn't make any sense at all," Groucho said. "But it wasn't trying to make sense, it was just trying to be funny." Unfortunately, *Humor Risk* suffered such a poor reception at its initial showing that the Marxes, spurred by the ever sensitive Groucho, destroyed all copies. To this day, film historians pray that a print of the Marx Brothers' first film will eventually turn up.

Groucho also tried his hand at love. As he declared in a monologue he wrote years later, he had a late start in dating: "I didn't go out with girls until I was 21 because my mother objected. After I was 21, the girls objected." Even then, he insisted, he had to have a chaperone. "You know what a chaperone is—that's a French word meaning 'Brother, are you in for a dull evening!'" Groucho's claims notwithstanding, shyness and an inordinately busy life probably had more to do with his lingering bachelorhood than Minnie had.

During the war, an 18-year-old woman named Ruth Johnson joined the act as Zeppo's dancing partner. "She was blonde and blue-eyed and weighed 118 well-distributed pounds," Groucho recalled. After several years of courtship, a judge married the couple at Chicago City Hall in 1920, when Groucho was a self-proclaimed "blushing 30." Even at such a momentous event, Groucho could not suppress his inborn irreverence. Throughout the ceremony, he ad-libbed his vows, including, "It may be holy to you, Judge, but we have other ideas."

4 "Hello, I Must Be Going"

ONE NIGHT DURING A performance of the smash Broadway run of *I'll Say She Is,* a brand new $6,000 Lincoln convertible was delivered to the front entrance of New York's Casino Theatre. Eager to try it out, its new owner decided to take it for a spin around the block, as he was not expected onstage for the show's Napoléon finale for at least another 10 minutes.

Groucho had not counted on traffic. Three blocks from the theater, he became caught between two trucks and was unable to move. Frantic, he left the car where it stood and, as best he could with his bulky Napoléon outfit, raced back to the theater. He finished the performance without a hitch, but when he returned to the spot where he had abandoned the Lincoln, it was gone. State police found it in Pennsylvania three months later, not too much the worse for wear, and delivered it to Groucho.

The grown-up Julius had a lot to learn about the real world. For two decades he and his brothers had been living a life on the road, working incessantly. They never stayed in one place long enough to own a car or a home. With the success of *I'll Say She Is,* Groucho, now approaching

---

In *Animal Crackers,* Captain Jeffrey T. Spaulding (Groucho) arrives at Mrs. Rittenhouse's (Margaret Dumont) posh mansion in a palanquin carried by Nubian slaves. Shortly after stepping from the palanquin Groucho utters one of his classic lines—"You're the most beautiful woman I've ever seen, which doesn't say much for you."

his mid-thirties, could finally slow down. He bought his first car (the Lincoln) and his first apartment, on Riverside Drive at 161st Street on New York's Upper West Side.

The brothers had become the toast of the town. They were invited to the most lavish parties in the show business world and moved in the most exclusive circles, including the rarefied world of New York's leading intellectuals, such as the humorist Robert Benchley, the writer Dorothy Parker, and the critic Alexander Woollcott, who had become one of the act's staunchest fans.

Woollcott, however, ignored Groucho—oddly taken a particular shine. Though a magical mime, Harpo was practically illiterate, whereas Groucho, through years of diligent reading, had become virtually as well read as Woollcott himself. Groucho craved acceptance by New York's intellectuals almost as much as success in show business. Whereas Harpo and Chico could impress the intelligentsia with their drinking, pool shooting, and card playing, Groucho—as he had had to do as a youth—had to rely on his lightning mind.

"He took to breaking into the conversation by twisting their pontifical statements around into jokes, or making outrageous puns from their big words," Arthur Marx wrote. While his father assured him, "They never caught on to me, they thought I was a great wit," the young Marx knew that the intellectuals' lukewarm reception of him always confounded Groucho.

All the uneasiness he felt in the presence of New York's cognoscenti, however, vanished before a Broadway audience. Although he often felt nervous before a performance—which evinced itself in insomnia and what he termed a "grippy feeling," consisting of cold feet and cigars that no longer tasted good—he was, said Arthur, "as relaxed on the stage as he was at home in his study, and as uninhibited as the worst extrovert."

Groucho's freewheeling stage style, backed up by his brothers' slapdash comedy, gained devoted fans by the minute in mid-1920s New York. As Groucho's friend, songwriter Harry Ruby, said in *The Marx Bros. Scrapbook,* "Their crazy kind of humor had never been seen before on Broadway." New York theatergoers, caught up in the mood of frivolity that swept the country under presidents Warren Harding and Calvin Coolidge, sopped up the Marx Brothers' special comic brew like a sponge.

On January 25, 1925, the brothers' second Broadway show, *The Cocoanuts,* opened at the Lyric Theatre on Forty-second Street. Their earlier shows, like most vaudeville acts, had contained a series of discrete, unconnected skits. But vaudeville and all its trappings had begun by this time to lose its luster with theatergoers, who preferred a single story. Groucho always strove to keep pace with changing times, so it is no accident that *The Cocoanuts* broke with Marxian tradition by bearing, as would all future Marx Brothers projects, one set of characters and one, albeit absurd, story line.

The Cocoanuts was a parody of the land boom then occurring in Florida. Groucho, in the lead role, played Henry W. Schlemmer, proprietor of the Cocoanuts, a seaside hotel in Cocoanut Beach. Schlemmer cuts a barely respectable figure who appears to be one step away from impoverishment. (As he says, "Three years ago I came to Florida without a nickel in my pocket. Now I have a nickel in my pocket.") Like many of Groucho's characters, Schlemmer is a con man who would be dangerous if he were not so bungling. His first concern is lining his own pockets—by selling substandard building lots to unsuspecting investors—but when push comes to shove, he plays the reluctant savior, helping to recover a stolen necklace and secretly furthering a love affair between one of his staff and a guest.

Groucho, Chico, and Harpo appear in a hotel scene from the 1929 movie *The Cocoanuts*. Originally a hit Broadway play, *The Cocoanuts* was a farce about would-be millionaires during the Florida land boom of the late 1920s.

The Cocoanuts had all the makings of a hit. It came fast on the heels of the hugely successful *I'll Say She Is*. It featured a cast of dozens, including several top vocalists and a line of talented chorus singers, and it had better sets than the slapped-together ones the Marx Brothers had scavenged for their earlier production. Finally, *The Cocoanuts* was written by one of the leading playwrights of the day, George S. Kaufman, with music and lyrics by Irving Berlin, who would soon become one of America's most beloved songwriters.

New York's hard-nosed critics did not let Groucho down. "I cannot recall ever having laughed more help-lessly, more flagrantly and more continuously in the theatre than I did at the way these Marxes carried on last evening," Woollcott wrote the day after the opening. "By the time Groucho Marx was rising to announce, 'The next number on the program will be a piccolo solo which we will omit' . . . we would have laughed at anything." Percy Hammond of the *New York Herald Tribune* also lauded Groucho that day. "Mr. Groucho Marx was the life of the party last night at the Lyric, affording more entertainment than did the librettist, the composer the chorus, and all the others, including his kinfolk," he wrote. "The major Marx is one of those gifted clowns who can make good jokes out of bad ones."

The Cocoanuts ran 377 performances on Broadway, then toured the country, including a special stop at the White House so the brothers could entertain Calvin Coolidge. Even for the president of the United States, Groucho could not suppress his natural inclination to affront. As he came onstage, Groucho glanced at Coolidge, who was known for taking four-hour naps every day, and said, "Aren't you up past your bedtime, Calvin?"

For Groucho, ad-libbing was par for the course, whether it added to existing lines or replaced them. He once excused his perpetual editing of scripts others had written for him by saying, "No matter how skillful the writer, there is a very personal rhythm to everyone's speech, and no one knows better what it is than the actor himself." Bored with repeating the same jokes night after night, Groucho worked in new material to such a degree that the original script often became all but unrecogniz-able. One night toward the end of the *Cocoanuts* tour, George Kaufman, who stood in the standing-room-only section of the theater quietly conversing with a friend, suddenly interrupted his companion to say, "I may be wrong, but I thought I just heard one of the original lines."

With the success of *The Cocoanuts,* Groucho settled down for good. He and Ruth now had two children, Arthur, born in 1921, and Miriam, born in 1927. Knowing from personal experience how difficult growing up in New York could be, he bought a 10-room home in the New York suburb of Great Neck, an exclusive hamlet on the north shore of Long Island. Groucho counted among his neighbors the writer Ring Lardner, the cartoonist Rube Goldberg, and the novelist F. Scott Fitzgerald, who later immortalized the town and its chic residents in his novel *The Great Gatsby.*

Yet Groucho did not move to Long Island to hobnob with luminaries. While Harpo and Chico persisted with their carefree lives, Groucho socialized only occasionally. "My idea of a good time is to lock myself in my room with a big Havana and read *The New Yorker,*" he once told his son. In Great Neck, he eased into the life of a country gentleman. When not working, he spent his time reading, playing the guitar, tending his fruit trees, entertaining friends, and playing with Arthur and Miriam. He particularly cherished reading—and embellishing—bedtime stories. "Generally he'd stick to the tried and true classics, but they weren't very true when he got through with them," Arthur recalled. "He'd keep the same story structure of the original, but it would be so full of jokes you'd hardly recognize it."

Even as Groucho retreated into his personal life, his stage fame grew. *The Cocoanuts* had been such a sensation that Sam Harris, the show's director, commissioned George Kaufman to draft a script for a new show. With help from a young writer named Morrie Ryskind, Kaufman wrote *Animal Crackers,* a musical comedy about a stolen painting and other misadventures at a posh party

A family photograph shows Groucho with his wife, Ruth, son, Arthur, and baby daughter, Miriam, around 1927. The Marxes lived in a 10-room home in Great Neck, a fashionable town on the north shore of New York's Long Island.

on Long Island. Groucho plays Captain Jeffrey T. Spaulding, a renowned explorer who is the honored guest at a reception being held at the palatial mansion of Mrs. Rittenhouse, a wealthy widow played by Margaret Dumont. In the opening scene, Captain Spaulding enters Mrs. Rittenhouse's front hall in a palanquin (a covered litter) shouldered by four Nubian slaves, who have accompanied him on his return from a recent expedition to Africa. He wears jodhpurs, knee-high boots, a bow tie, and a pith helmet, as well as his usual facial getup. ("Soon all your everyday African explorers were dressing this way," he jested.)

When Captain Spaulding asks how much he owes his bearers and they utter a mumbled response, he replies, "That's an outrage. I could have got a Yellow Cab for a buck and a quarter." Groucho then turns to his statuesque hostess and, with the assembled guests providing a chorus, begins a song, "Hooray for Captain Spaulding":

> Hello, I must be going.
> I cannot stay, I only
> Came to say,
> I must be going.
> I'll stay a week or two,
> I'll stay the summer through,
> But I am telling you,
> I must be going.

The tune, written by songsters Bert Kalmar and Harry Ruby, became Groucho's most famous. It later served as the theme music for his hit television show, "You Bet Your Life." The scene itself, immortalized on film, also remains his best known. While he sings, Groucho dances a wild whirligig that still has audiences roaring today, and he later utters some of his most often quoted lines, including, "One morning I shot an elephant in my pajamas. How he got in my pajamas, I don't know." At one point, Captain Spaulding proposes marriage simultaneously to Mrs. Rittenhouse and another stately woman.

"Why, that's bigamy!" exclaims Mrs. Rittenhouse.

"Yes, and it's big-a-me, too," Captain Spaulding responds, leering at the dumbfounded dowagers and wiggling his thickly painted eyebrows.

As in all Marx Brothers efforts, Chico and Harpo superbly complement their younger brother's wit

(Zeppo, sadly, always played the odd man out). By now Chico had perfected his "Eye-talian" character, which in *Animal Crackers* becomes Signor Emanuel Ravelli, one of the musicians hired to entertain Mrs. Rittenhouse's party. His verbal duel with Captain Spaulding is one of many the two brothers "fought" throughout their coupled career:

Spaulding: What do you get an hour?
Ravelli: For playing, we get-a ten dollars an hour.
Spaulding: I see. What do you get for not playing?
Ravelli: Twelve dollars an hour. Now for rehearsing, we make special rates. That's-a fifteen dollars an hour.
Spaulding: And what do you get for not rehearsing?
Ravelli: You couldn't afford it. You see, if we don't rehearse, we don't a-play. And if we don't a-play, that runs into money.
Spaulding: How much would you want to run into an open manhole?
Ravelli: Just-a the cover charge.
Spaulding: Well, drop in some time.
Ravelli: Sewer.

Harpo, as the professor, is even zanier. *Animal Crackers* features "a piece of business"—as Groucho called a routine—that Harpo developed back in his vaudeville days along with other props, such as his old-fashioned taxi horn, which sufficed for a voice. The routine appears in the finale, when Harpo comes up with the stolen painting (as well as two fakes). As the guests gather around, a detective, who has come to investigate the theft, asks the wide-eyed Harpo if he is ready to give up a life of crime. Harpo nods, and the policeman begins pumping his hand enthusiastically. As they shake, a table knife drops from Harpo's sleeve, then another, and another, until *several hundred* knives lie on the floor at his feet. After a pause, Captain Spaulding remarks, "I can't understand what's delaying the coffee pot." Just then a silver coffeepot tumbles from Harpo's sleeve.

Like *The Cocoanuts, Animal Crackers* received glowing reviews the morning after it opened. On October 24, 1928, in the *New York Herald Tribune,* Percy Hammond again raved about Groucho: "That unruly clown jumps blandly [suavely] through the paper hoops of the libretto, and as he does so he adds substantially to our sum of nonsense." Groucho acted the role of Captain Spaulding 191 times on Broadway.

Meanwhile, in early 1929, the Marx Brothers began filming a screen version of *The Cocoanuts* in Paramount Pictures' East Coast studios in nearby Astoria, Queens. Except for Wednesdays and Saturdays, when they had matinees, the foursome spent

most of 1929 shooting *The Cocoanuts* during the day and acting *Animal Crackers* at night. Indeed, they missed the premiere of their new film at the Rialto Theatre on Forty-second Street and Broadway because they were performing their new stage show just two blocks away at the Forty-fourth Street Theatre. The juxtaposition caused Groucho to occasionally mix up his lines, but no one could fudge his way through a few bungled deliveries better than Julius H. Marx.

In a scene from the film *Animal Crackers,* a policeman confronts Captain Spaulding (Groucho), Mrs. Rittenhouse (Margaret Dumont), and Horatio Jameson (Zeppo). Originally based on the musical play by Morrie Ryskind and George Kaufman, *Animal Crackers* proved to be the perfect vehicle for Groucho's fast-paced, ad-libbed puns.

The film version of *The Cocoanuts* set several records. It was the first musical ever filmed, one of the only filmed records of a 1920s musical comedy, and one of the first sound movies. As Paul Zimmerman and Burt Goldblatt wrote in their book *The Marx Brothers at the Movies,* "*Cocoanuts* is one of those happy accidents of art and technology in which cinema found sound just in time to give full voice to Groucho's wit, Chico's verbal tenacity, and Harpo's silence." Groucho might have disagreed about the "full voice." While filming, the brothers had to speak directly at a potted plant, where technicians had hidden the studio's bulky, inefficient microphones. Though it went against their very nature, the Marx Brothers also had to stand practically still, because the five movie cameras used in the filming could not pan to

follow an actor's movements as they can today. As a result, in *The Cocoanuts,* the brothers come across as being rather stiff.

Nevertheless, the movie fared so well that Groucho and his brothers soon signed a contract with Paramount to do four more films. The next movie, not surprisingly,

Groucho proudly poses with his new Packard convertible in 1929. In October 1929, Groucho experienced two catastrophes: the stock market crashed, taking with it all of his savings, and his beloved mother, Minnie, died.

was *Animal Crackers,* but that was the last film made from a Marx Brothers act, because they never again put together a stage show. The reason was purely financial. While Groucho earned $2,000 a week for performing on Broadway, he made $50,000 per picture, which entailed just a few months of shooting.

Animal Crackers, released in 1930, was as big a hit in the movies as it had been on the stage. *Film Daily,* the business journal of the movie industry, put it succinctly: "While most of the repartee is nonsense, it gets laughs, and that's what counts."

As 1929 dawned, Groucho, like many Americans, lived more comfortably than he ever had. During the previous eight years, he had reaped some of the benefits of the most spectacular economic boom the country had yet seen. By the late 1920s, one Model T car came off the assembly line every 10 seconds, and eager consumers snatched up nifty new appliances, such as telephones, toasters, and vacuum cleaners, almost as fast as they hit store shelves.

With his stage and film earnings, Groucho traded in the Lincoln for a racy new Packard convertible—complete with wire wheels and rumble seat—and bought a Cord car for his wife, Ruth, as well. He paid $5,000 to join an exclusive Long Island club. (Later, upon resigning from another fancy club, he wrote, "Gentlemen: Please accept my resignation. I don't care to belong to any organization that will accept me as a member.") By the fall of 1929, he had saved up $240,000, which he kept in what most people at the time considered the safest place: the stock market.

Even movie stars can have bad breaks, and two came for Groucho that fall. First, on October 24, the stock market collapsed, ushering in the Great Depression and swallowing Groucho's hard-earned nest egg. Second, Minnie died. She not only had been a loving mother but had launched Groucho in show business. "Without her there would never have been the Marx Brothers," Groucho wrote in *The Secret Word Is Groucho*. "She was manipulative and intrusive and the stage mother of them all. She was also a great woman." Woollcott, who had by now become a close family friend, agreed. "Of the people I have met," he wrote in a eulogy in the *New Yorker*, "I would name her as among the few of whom it could be said they had greatness."

Groucho sought to put such painful memories behind him as soon as possible. He did it symbolically one day in 1929, after playing the 18th hole at California's famed Pebble Beach golf course. In a silent admission of his years-long failure to improve his golf game, Groucho calmly walked to the edge of the cliff overlooking the Pacific and dropped each of his remaining golf balls over the brink. Without a word, he then heaved his bag of clubs over the edge and strolled back to his hotel, "as lighthearted," wrote Arthur, "as if he had just been reprieved from the gallows."

5 "Unsquelchable Effrontery"

FOR MOST AMERICANS, the early 1930s was a time of great hardship. Companies went out of business in droves, leaving one of four workers out of a job. Tens of thousands of people in the Great Plains, where the dust bowl aggravated the depression's effects by laying once-fertile soil to waste, migrated in desperation to California. The worst poverty the country had ever known brought a boom, paradoxically, in crime, with gangsters like Bonnie and Clyde getting away, literally, with murder.

Groucho, however, was little affected by the Great Depression. He quickly began to rebuild the savings he lost in the crash by making one Marx Brothers movie a year, each bringing him $50,000. So solvent had he become by 1931 that the normally thrifty Groucho treated his family to a Royal Suite cruise to England.

Groucho went to London to star with his brothers in a show called *Charles Cochran's Varieties*. Playing at that city's Palace Theatre, the *Varieties* featured 10 different acts, of which the finale was the Marx Brothers. Groucho, Chico, Harpo, and Zeppo chose a selection of scenes from *The Cocoanuts* and *Animal*

With cigar in hand, Groucho dances with Lucille (Thelma Todd), a mobster's girlfriend, on board a cruise ship in *Monkey Business*. Groucho plays a shyster lawyer and stowaway in the 1931 hit film, which was the first Marx Brothers movie written specifically for the screen.

Crackers. Although one critic felt that the translation from film to stage must have been done "by a blind man with a pair of blunt scissors," most reviewers raved. Theater critic E. A. Baughan wrote that "when Groucho first came on the stage at the Palace Theatre last night the audience roared at him," while another commentator held that Groucho "hurls more fun and puns at you in two minutes than most comedians would dare deliver in an hour."

On his return from England, Groucho moved to Hollywood to shoot the final three films in the Marxes' Paramount contract. Despite the dismal situation in most of the country, Hollywood remained a bastion of extravagant living. "Taxes were still nominal, and Hollywood's queens and kings lived far more luxuriously than most of the reigning families in Europe," Groucho wrote. "Most of them tossed their money around as though they manufactured it themselves in the cellar." Whereas his brothers leaped into the Hollywood social scene with panache, Groucho largely restricted his socializing to the Hillcrest Country Club in Beverly Hills. There he often dined at the Comedians' Round Table with leading funnymen like Charlie Chaplin, W. C. Fields, and Jack Benny.

As always, his family remained all-important to him. In 1933, Groucho, Ruth, Arthur, and Miriam moved into a 14-room mansion on North Hillcrest Road in Beverly Hills. While Chico, Harpo, and Zeppo hobnobbed with some of the biggest names in Hollywood, Groucho preferred a quiet evening with his wife and children.

The marquees of the Palace Theatre and RKO's Mayfair Theatre illuminate New York's Broadway at night in 1930. The Marx Brothers' performances received rave reviews from most critics; similarly, their film appearances gleaned glowing commentary from reviewers.

When he did go out in public, Groucho loved to conceal his identity. Without his glasses and greasepaint, he became incognito. "I had it both ways," he once confided to Arthur, "stardom on stage and anonymity in everyday life." When he arrived with his family at a restaurant at which he had invariably neglected to make a reservation, Groucho would say to the maître d', who did not recognize him, "I'm Jackson, of the Stonewall Jacksons, this is Mrs. Jackson, and these are all the little Jacksons." When Ruth urged him to give his real name, which likely would have gained them a table immediately, Groucho would turn again to the maître d' and sigh, "My wife wants me to tell you who I am. My name's not really Jackson. It's Schwartz, and I'm in the wholesale plumbing supply business. And this is Mrs. Schwartz and all the little Schwartzes."

Sometimes Groucho's playfulness landed the Marxes in hot water. When their cruise ship sailed into New York harbor on their return from Europe in 1931, Groucho decided to have a little fun with the customs form:

Name: Julius H. Marx
Address: 21 Lincoln Road, Great Neck, L.I.
Born: Yes.
Hair: Not much.
Occupation: Smuggler.
List items purchased out of the U.S., where bought, and the purchase price: Wouldn't you like to know?

Not amused, and not knowing whom they were dealing with, the customs agents detained the Marxes while they painstakingly searched their belongings. During this process, Groucho, still in a jocular mood, whispered to Ruth in a voice loud enough for the agents to hear, "What did you do with the opium?" "That was all the Customs Inspector needed to hear," Arthur recalled. The family was shuffled off to another room, separated by sex, and strip-searched.

Harpo, Groucho, Chico, and Zeppo pose with their father, Simon "Frenchie" Marx, during the shooting of *Monkey Business*. This was one of the last times Frenchie and his sons appeared together in a photograph.

Fittingly, Groucho's next film character was a stowaway on a cruise ship sailing from Europe to America. The film was *Monkey Business,* released in 1931. In it he portrays a shyster lawyer who hitches a free ride along with three other stowaways (played, of course, by Chico, Harpo, and Zeppo). *Monkey Business* features the brothers' usual brand of Marxism: Chico is the money-

grubbing Italian, Harpo the nearly out-of-control mute, and Zeppo the handsome lover who courts a young singer on board. Groucho himself woos the girlfriend of a mobster: "I know, I know, you're a woman who's been getting nothing but dirty breaks," he croons after sneaking into the woman's stateroom to hide from the ship's officers. "Well, we can clean and tighten your brakes, but you'll have to stay in the garage all night."

Such clever lines pepper the script, which was cowritten by Will B. Johnstone, who wrote *I'll Say She Is,* and S. J. Perelman, one of America's preeminent humorists. Perelman's influence can be felt "in the highly literate script, in the beautifully honed edge on Groucho's puns, in the methodical madness and mordant tone of the film," wrote Paul Zimmerman and Burt Goldblatt. So witty are Groucho's lines that British prime minister Winston Churchill, himself one of the century's wittiest men, watched the film to take his mind off the German bombing of London during World War II. "I was glad of the diversion," he said. Critics appreciated the film as well. "Suffice it to say," wrote Mordaunt Hall of the *New York Times,* "that few persons will be able to go to the Rivoli

[Theater] and keep a straight face."

Perelman and Johnstone went on to collaborate on the Marx Brothers' next film. Released in 1932, *Horse Feathers* is a satire of American education whose unabashed irreverence owes a lot to *Fun in Hi Skule*. Groucho plays Professor Quincy Adams Wagstaff, the new president of Huxley College, whose main charge is to produce a winning football team. Perelman's wit shines through Groucho right from the opening scene, when the former president tries to introduce Groucho to the assembled faculty and students: "Now that you've stepped into my shoes . . . ," the ex-president begins. "Oh, so that's what I stepped into," Groucho interrupts, glancing at his soles. "If these are your shoes, the least you could do was have them cleaned."

Throughout the film, Groucho relies on "unsquelchable effrontery," as *Time* magazine once described his innate talent, to lampoon every aspect of higher learning. The finale, in which the four brothers play football against 11 giants from the opposing team, rests squarely in the Marx Brothers annals as one of their all-time zaniest skits. During the scene, Groucho pauses for a moment from wooing a woman in the grandstand to tackle an opposing player on his way to a touchdown. "That'll teach him to pass a lady without tipping his hat," he observes.

Horse Feathers' outdoor scene was one of several cinematic firsts for the brothers, including more spacious sets and action that could only reasonably happen on film, such as a scene in which Chico and Harpo fall through a ceiling into the middle of a bridge game. But basically the film is vintage, vaudeville-inspired Marx Brothers. "The business of reviewing a Marx Brothers film need consist of saying little more than whether or not the boys are keeping to their stride," reported Richard Watts of the *New York Herald Tribune* after the film's opening on

August 10, 1932. "Any effort to tell too much about their latest conventions will result only in confusion for the reviewer and the picture." William Bocknell of the New York *Telegram* said simply, "I laughed last night as I have seldom laughed before." Five days after the film's opening, the Marx Brothers—wearing their football uniforms and scrunched together in a metal garbage can—appeared on the cover of *Time* magazine.

Harpo reacts to the opposing players in a college football game in the 1932 madcap comedy, *Horse Feathers*.

Having perfected his art, Groucho now began to branch out into other media. In 1930 he published his first book, *Beds,* a playful look at love. Because it reached bookstores during the depression, sales were weak. "Instead of buying my book, people took to their own," Groucho lamented. In 1933, he and Chico did an NBC radio series called "Flywheel, Shyster, and Flywheel." Groucho portrayed Waldorf T. Flywheel, senior partner in an ambulance-chasing law firm; Chico played his assistant. Sponsored by Standard Oil of New Jersey, the show ran for only 26 weeks. Clearly, despite Groucho's piquancy and peerless delivery, for many people much of the Marx Brothers' humor remained visual.

The public did not have to wait long for another eyeful of the Marx Brothers. *Duck Soup,* their final film for Paramount Pictures, came out in 1933. Set in the fic-

In the 1933 film *Duck Soup,* which many considered to be the Marx Brothers' masterpiece, Groucho plays Rufus T. Firefly, the new "dictator" of the fictional duchy of Freedonia. The movie was a barely concealed attack on the political situation in Europe at the time, specifically the rise of fascism and national socialism in Italy and Germany.

tional country of Freedonia, *Duck Soup* is a thinly veiled attack on fascism and other forms of authoritarian government. At the time *Duck Soup* appeared, Adolf Hitler's fiery nationalistic speeches were being rebroadcast in the United States, to the consternation of democratic Americans. "Harpo responded in his private life by changing his name from Adolph to Arthur," remarked Paul Zimmerman and Burt Goldblatt. "The brothers responded with *Duck Soup*." So well did the film strike its political mark that Benito Mussolini, the Italian fascist leader, later denounced the Marx Brothers and ordered his subjects not to laugh at them.

Groucho played Rufus T. Firefly, the new president of Freedonia, whose former corrupt rulers ran the kingdom into bankruptcy. Firefly is a bungler who admits, "If you think this country's bad off now, just wait 'til I get through with it." When one of his cabinet members hands him a document and asks him if it is clear, he says, "Why, a four-year-old child could understand this report." He then turns to his secretary (Zeppo) and whispers, "Go out and get a four-year-old child. I can't make head or tail of it."

The multimillionairess Mrs. Teasdale (Margaret Dumont) hires Firefly to return the country to the heights it enjoyed under her late husband, Mr. Teasdale. As usual, Groucho has things under his own haphazard control:

> *Firefly:* Not that I care, but where is your husband?
> *Mrs. Teasdale:* Why, he's dead.
> *Firefly:* I bet he's just using that as an excuse.
> *Mrs. Teasdale:* I was with him till the end.
> *Firefly:* No wonder he passed away.
> *Mrs. Teasdale:* I held him in my arms and kissed him.
> *Firefly:* Oh, I see, then it was murder. Will you marry me? Did he leave you any money? Answer the second question first.

During the 1930s, the Marx Brothers pose with American baseball great Lou Gehrig, the "Iron Horse" of the New York Yankees.

Mrs. Teasdale: He left me his entire fortune.

Firefly: Is that so? Can't you see what I'm trying to tell you? I love you.

Fans became as devoted to such priceless repartee between Groucho and Margaret Dumont as they were to

Harpo's capers or Chico's shoot-the-keys piano solos. Like the brothers' characters, Dumont's role came straight out of vaudeville, which often featured an actress depicting a rich widow. Dumont played the role to perfection because she *was* a rich widow—of sugar heir John Muller, Jr.—and because she never understood Groucho's witticisms. When Firefly's rudeness brings Freedonia to war with neighboring Sylvania, Firefly exhorts his brothers, "Remember, we're fighting for this woman's honor, which is probably more than she ever did." After shooting the scene, Dumont asked Groucho to explain the joke. Dumont appeared in so many Marx Brothers films— seven—that many consider her an honorary Marx brother. (She played similar roles in films starring comedians W. C. Fields, Jack Benny, and Laurel and Hardy.) "She was a wonderful woman and a fine actress," Groucho said after Dumont died in 1965. "I loved her."

Dumont played the foil to Groucho so expertly that she unwittingly stole Zeppo's fire. Though Groucho considered his youngest sibling the wittiest of them all offstage, Zeppo joined the act too late, after his three older brothers had already formed solid characters. Somehow there was no room for a fourth. As such, Zeppo's straight characters always seemed ill formed, and he knew it. *Duck Soup,* Groucho said, was Zeppo's last course. He left the act to become a theatrical producer and, later, a manufacturer of airplane parts.

Today, Marx Brothers purists consider *Duck Soup* the brothers' masterwork. (Along with the later *A Night at the Opera,* it is housed in the film classics library at New York's Museum of Modern Art.) The Marx Brothers were at the top of their form. As *Duck Soup* demonstrates so well, their appeal lies in their eagerness to act on one's most forbidden desires. As Roger Manwell wrote in *Film* about *Duck Soup,* "They represent all the things that one was brought up not to do." Nothing lies outside the range of their biting satire. With equal impunity, they target power, wealth, authority, class, politics, sex, education, and war. And they do it with a refreshing blend of innocence and maturity. The London *Times* said it succinctly:

> There are other funny men. There are other musicians of accomplishment. There are other fantastics. What makes these great clowns is this combination of fun and fantasy with something else, a mixture of worldly wisdom and naïveté, of experience but also of an innocence never altogether lost, of dignity and absurdity together, so that for a moment we love and applaud mankind.

Yet, ironically, *Duck Soup* opened to poor reviews. "The Marx Brothers take something of a nose-dive," declaimed John S. Cohen, Jr., in the *New York Sun* after the film's opening on November 17, 1933. The *Los Angeles Times* chose the pejorative Groucho feared most: "washed up."

In the first months of 1934, the film's disappointing box office performance threatened the Marx Brothers' career. Their fame reached its lowest ebb since their return from England 12 years before. Rather than mope about waiting for a film offer that might never come, Groucho acted a straight role—his first—in the summer theater in Skowhegan, Maine. The play was *Twentieth Century,* based on the life of the theatrical producer Jed Harris. As the summer progressed, he and his brothers began to wonder if their lives in show business were over. Then Chico, who George Kaufman once claimed possessed an "odd combination of business acumen and financial idiocy," again came through.

6 Exhaustingly Funny

ONE AFTERNOON in the fall of 1934, Groucho, winding up his stage appearance in *Twentieth Century*, received the telephone call he had unconsciously been awaiting all year. It was Chico, phoning from California: Irving Thalberg had invited the Marx Brothers to lunch.

Thalberg was a bright young producer at Metro-Goldwyn-Mayer (M-G-M), one of the largest Hollywood studios. A thin, frail man of 37, he had already become head of production at M-G-M. During a bridge game, Thalberg had casually asked Chico how the Marx Brothers were faring. Rather than admit the truth, the ever cool Chico simply had said they were between films. Thalberg then had requested that he gather his brothers for a luncheon at the Beverly Wilshire hotel. There, the brothers hit it off with Thalberg, who by meal's end had offered to produce the sixth Marx Brothers picture, *A Night at the Opera*.

In the film, Groucho plays Otis B. Driftwood, a sly entrepreneur who agrees to help the rich dowager Mrs. Claypool (Margaret Dumont) make her place in society by contributing $200,000 to the New York Opera. The film

A poster announces M-G-M's *A Night at the Opera* in 1935. Thanks to Chico, producer Irving Thalberg became interested in making the Marx Brothers' sixth film, which would eventually outsell all other Marx Brothers efforts at the box office.

features some of the Marx Brothers' most celebrated moments on celluloid, including a scene where 20 people cram into Groucho's tiny stateroom on board ship.

Thalberg stopped at nothing to make *A Night at the Opera* the best Marx Brothers film ever, and many fans feel it even eclipses *Duck Soup* as the greatest film the brothers did. First, Thalberg brought back the tried-and-true writing team of George Kaufman and Morrie Ryskind—scriptwriters for the movies and *Animal Crackers*—and threw in for good measure a comic writer named Al Boasberg, who many people at the time considered the funniest man alive.

Second, Thalberg felt strongly that comedy should further the plot, not the other way around as had been the case in all previous Marx Brothers films. He made sure there was something for everyone in the picture: romance, a hit song ("Alone"), a solid if inane plot, and, of course, plenty of good, old-fashioned Marx Brothers slapstick. Third, he hired a painstaking director, Sam Wood, who often shot scenes 20 or 30 times to get them just right.

Thalberg's brainstorm was to take the new show on the road before filming it. The Marx Brothers grew up honing their material before live audiences, but of their five films, only *The Cocoanuts* and *Animal Crackers* had been given the stamp of approval from hundreds of audiences. Touring *A Night at the Opera* gave Groucho and his brothers a chance to test their lines—and Thalberg to delete any that failed to bring laughs.

In early 1935, the Marxes performed a stage version of *A Night at the Opera* four times a day in four western U.S. cities: Salt Lake City, Utah; Seattle, Washington; Portland, Oregon; and Santa Barbara, California. Kaufman and Ryskind sat in the audience, timing the laughs. This proved invaluable, for the show in this early, rough-edged form "laid one of the biggest eggs in the history of the

Marx Brothers, if not all show business," wrote Arthur Marx. But by the time the tour ended, the brothers reportedly returned with 175 surefire lines.

The film opened on November 15, 1935, and was an instant sensation. Thorton Delehanty of the *New York Post* echoed the sentiment of critics and viewers alike when he wrote that nothing the Marx Brothers had done to date was "as consistently and exhaustingly funny or as rich in comic invention and satire as *Opera*."

So successful was the film—it turned a $3-million profit, then unprecedented for a Marx Brothers movie—that Thalberg immediately initiated another film, *A Day at the Races*. Since Kaufman had returned to New York, Thalberg hired three new writers. But he kept as much of the *Opera* formula as possible, signing on Sam Wood as director and Al Boasberg as gagman. Again he toured the brothers, whose stagehands passed out cards to audience members asking for their responses to specific lines.

In *A Day at the Races* (released in 1937), Groucho plays Dr. Hugo Z. Hackenbush, a horse doctor who masquerades as a physician to Mrs. Emily Upjohn (Margaret Dumont), a patient in a sanatorium. Unless the sanatorium's young owner (Maureen O'Sullivan) can raise enough money to pay the mortgage, she will be forced to sell to the owner of a local racetrack, who wants to convert the asylum into a casino. Mrs. Upjohn, with her millions, is the only one who can save it, but she plans to leave the hospital because its doctors refuse to find anything wrong with her. When Hackenbush turns up at her request, she proudly announces to the sanatorium's distinguished medical experts, "I never knew there was anything wrong with me until I met him." In the end, after the usual Marx Brothers horseplay—and against all reason—Hackenbush saves the sanatorium, and its owner marries a young suitor.

In the notorious stateroom scene of *A Night at the Opera,* entrepreneur Otis B. Driftwood (Groucho) finds his room overflowing with people. In the story, Fiorello (Chico) tries to further the career of a young tenor, Riccardo Baroni (Allan Jones, seen here with suspenders), and Driftwood tries to con wealthy Mrs. Claypool (Margaret Dumont) into investing her fortune in an opera company.

With their previous masterpiece, *A Night at the Opera,* Thalberg not only revived the Marx Brothers but brought them more acclaim than ever. So it was a blow to all of them when, three weeks into the filming of *A Day at the Races,* he died of pneumonia. So enamored had Groucho become of Thalberg that after his death in 1936, Groucho claimed his interest in making movies waned. Though their association had been brief, its sudden end symbolized, for Groucho, the end of an era, a feeling compounded by the death of his father, Frenchie, the same year.

It comes as no surprise, then, that the Marx Brothers' next picture, *Room Service,* a farce set in a New York City hotel, is widely regarded as their weakest effort. *Room Service* had all the earmarks of a hit (and, ironically, it reaped enthusiastic reviews upon its release in 1938): their veteran collaborator Morrie Ryskind adapted the screenplay from a hit Broadway play, the screen rights to which RKO Radio Pictures, the producer, had purchased for the then record price of $225,000. But for the first time in the Marx Brothers' career, the material had not been written specifically for them, and that was the film's fatal flaw. "We can't do gags or play characters that aren't ours," said Groucho, who played Gordon Miller, a theatrical producer who will stop at nothing to keep his play alive. "We tried it, and we'll never do it again."

After *Room Service,* the Marx Brothers returned to M-G-M and shot three films in rapid succession. *At the Circus,* in which Groucho played J. Cheever Loophole, an unscrupulous lawyer who comes to the rescue of a failing circus, appeared in 1939. In 1940, *Go West* came out, with Groucho playing S. Quentin Quale, a man out to seek his fortune in the West during the gold rush of the late 1840s. Margaret Dumont, whom fans had come to consider the fourth Marx Brother, was conspicuous by her absence. But she returned in *The Big Store,* released in 1941. As Martha Phelps, Dumont learns that the manager of the department store that her nephew owns plans to kill her nephew, marry her, and thus gain full ownership. Mrs. Phelps calls in private detective Wolf J. Flywheel (Groucho) to save the day.

"The pleasure in the late M-G-M movies, and there's plenty, lies in the solid fulfillment of expectations," said Paul Zimmerman and Burt Goldblatt about these three films. The movies offer classic Marx Brothers, and on the whole they were well received. Groucho utters many a memorable line—the best, as usual, with Dumont, his screen love of more than a decade. "Judge Chanock will sit on my left hand and you will sit on my right hand," Dumont informs Groucho at a dinner in *At the Circus.* "How will you eat," he responds, "through a tube?" Or in *The Big Store:* "I'm afraid that after we're married awhile, a beautiful girl will come along and you'll forget all about me," Dumont murmurs. "Don't be silly," replies Groucho. "I'll write you twice a week."

During the shooting of *The Big Store,* Groucho turned 50. The brothers were past their peak, and all three were growing tired of the nonstop pace that had resulted in 10 films in 12 years. Some critics, too, grew blasé about the Marx Brothers' unique species of tomfoolery. In his review of *At the Circus,* for instance, Howard Barnes of the *New York Herald Tribune* wrote that the brothers "whip up some passages of high hilarity, but there is no sustained comic note in their new offering." By the time *The Big Store* appeared, the Marx Brothers had decided it would be their last film.

"When I say we're sick of the movies," Groucho told a reporter at the time, "what I mean is that the people are about to get sick of us. By getting out now, we're anticipating public demand and by a very short margin. Our stuff is stale, and so are we." Critics agreed. "This swan song of the Marx Brothers," wrote Leo Mishkin about *The Big Store* in the New York *Morning Telegraph,* "is just a hodge-podge knockabout farce, bearing little relation, either actual or spiritual, to the past."

In early 1942, after more than 30 years as a team, the Marx Brothers disbanded. "The Marx Brothers as a team were officially *phfft,*" Groucho wrote. "We went our separate ways: I got custody of the moustache, Harpo kept the blond wig, and Chico bought a new Buick." Groucho was glad to be out. As he confided to his friend Arthur Sheekman during the filming of *The Big Store,* "I'm happy to escape from this kind of picture, for the character I'm playing now I find wholly repulsive. Acting in the movies no longer interests me."

Later that year, Groucho broke up another long-lasting union when he divorced Ruth after 21 years of marriage, claiming their life together had become "untenable." Ruth had become an alcoholic, so Groucho gained custody of Miriam, who was then in her mid-teens (Arthur, an aspiring professional tennis player, was away on tour). "The house is pretty quiet with just Miriam and me rattling around the 14 rooms," Groucho wrote to Arthur after Ruth moved out. "Well, it's better than 14 people rattling around two rooms. I'll let things drift along—anyway, for the present."

Following the two breakups, Groucho immersed himself in his work, as he had done in previous hard times. His career outside of the movies moved along briskly. In 1937, he cowrote a screenplay for a movie entitled *The King and the Chorus Girl,* which *Life* magazine praised as "easily the season's silliest movie." He also continued writing articles for various magazines, including his favorite, the *New Yorker.* These pieces reveal that, although prominent writers like George Kaufman and S. J. Perelman created most of the jokes he told so expertly on film, Groucho was no slouch as a comic writer. In an article for *This Week, USA* called "My Best Friend Is a Dog," Groucho said he missed his pet so much whenever he visited New York on business that "when I see a girl with a pretty dog in the hotel lobby, tears come into my eyes and I invite the pup into the lounge for a drink." In another article, "Groucho Marx Turns Himself in for Scrap," Groucho suggests that had humans been built scientifically, there would be no need for mouths. "You naturally ask, 'How would we eat?' Frankly, I don't know, but I'll give it some thought over the weekend."

In 1941, Groucho published his second book, *Many Happy Returns,* a humorous take on taxes. The jacket copy, which could not have been penned by anyone except Groucho himself, explains that the book was written during a sandstorm at Palm Springs and started out as a serious novel. "Sand kept flying into Mr. Marx's typewriter. To his surprise, he discovered that the finished manuscript was a book on the income tax." The jacket wrap went on to give a brief biography of the author: "Always precocious, Groucho Marx, author, actor, and tax wizard, was born in Manhattan at the age of five. He was immediately signed up as a member of the Four Marx Brothers."

Many Happy Returns contains the usual Groucho tomfoolery. He wrote that Clark Gable only made two films a year with his on-screen lover Lana Turner because "he knows that every time he kisses Miss Turner, the govern-

Groucho kicks up his heels with actress Veronica Lake during a performance for American GIs in World War II. Groucho helped raise $40 million for the wartime effort in 1942.

ment gets sixty percent." Groucho goes on with his characteristic wit:

> Do you suppose Casanova could have been hotfooting it around Europe so successfully if he had his mind on taxes? Take any of the great lovers of history—Lord Byron, Abelard, or Cesar Romero; they have made a success of love only because they have lived love. They were not thinking of Schedule B and Tax Item 7 when responding to *la grande passion* ("love" to you and the rest of the family. P.S. I expect to be home for the holidays).

Groucho also kept up his fledgling career in radio. In the late 1930s, he had teamed up with Chico again to do a weekly radio show called *That Was the Week That Was.* On the air, Groucho assumed the role of Ulysses S. Drivvle, eagle-eyed newshound; Chico was his trusty assistant Penelli. Like their first radio show together, "Flywheel, Shyster, and Flywheel," it ran for only half a year. In the early 1940s, Groucho made guest appearances on radio; then in 1943 he briefly landed his own program, a weekly coast-to-coast variety show called "Blue Ribbon Town," sponsored by Pabst Beer.

While Groucho kept busy throughout the 1930s, the world slowly slid toward war. Two insidious forces worked in tandem to undermine the fragile peace that had held sway since World War I: the Great Depression, which unleashed global economic misery, and the rise of totalitarian, militaristic regimes, such as the Nazis in Germany and the Fascists in Italy. In 1939, Germany invaded Poland, and World War II began. The United States, caught up in a spirit of isolationism spawned during the boom years of the 1920s, managed to stay out of the war until December 7, 1941, when Japanese bombers destroyed a U.S. naval base in a surprise attack at Pearl Harbor, Hawaii. For the next four years, more than 11 million Americans fought in the most devastating war the world had yet known.

Although he was too old to fight, Groucho served his country in his own way. For several years he toured the nation, giving solo stand-up comedy routines at army camps and, later, veterans' hospitals. Unlike his failed farm venture, Groucho's fund-raising efforts paid off in spades. By the time a bandwagon of Hollywood stars that he joined in 1942 had reached Minneapolis, Minnesota, on a cross-country tour, it had raised $40 million for the wartime government of President Franklin D. Roosevelt.

In the midst of the tour, on April 30, 1942, Groucho visited the White House as a guest of Roosevelt's wife, Eleanor. He had accepted the invitation with alacrity, because for him, as for many people in show business at the time, "getting Roosevelt reelected in 1944 was as much a part of the war effort as any of the camp shows we'd done." Throughout his life, Groucho was a staunch Democrat. "I frankly find Democrats a better, more sympathetic crowd," he once wrote. "It's been said often before, and until I have greater evidence to the contrary, I'll continue to believe that Democrats have greater regard for the common man than Republicans do." Even though he had achieved fame and fortune, he had not forgotten his humble roots.

Groucho did not remain solo for long, either personally or professionally. Three years after he divorced Ruth, he married Catherine "Kay" Gorcey, a 21-year-old aspiring actress with whom he had a daughter, Melinda, in 1946. That same year, less than five years after they disbanded, the Marx Brothers reunited for the film *A Night in Casablanca.*

When Warner Brothers, producer of the smash 1943 film *Casablanca,* learned of the proposed title for the Marx Brothers' new film, its lawyers demanded that another name be chosen. In true irrepressible style, Groucho fired back a reply, saying he could not understand the company's attitude: "Even if you plan on

re-releasing your picture, I am sure that the average movie fan could learn in time to distinguish between Ingrid Bergman [*Casablanca*'s heroine] and Harpo. I don't know whether I could, but I certainly would like to try." After several more letters containing similar balderdash, a bewildered Warner Brothers legal staff backed down.

Groucho married aspiring actress Catherine "Kay" Gorcey on July 21, 1945, in Hollywood. A year later they had a daughter, Melinda, but the marriage was dissolved in 1950.

In *A Night in Casablanca,* Groucho plays Ronald Cornblow, the new manager of the Casablanca Hotel, a seedy establishment whose managers have an unfortunate habit of being poisoned at lunch. Cornblow tries to run things his way and only gets into trouble. The lines he delivers along the way have none of the crisp irreverence of those uttered in his previous incarnations. To wit: "You know, I think you're the most beautiful woman in the whole world," he says to a new arrival. "Do you really?" she responds. "No, but I don't mind lying if it'll get me somewhere." Groucho suffered when lines scripted for him fell short of his rigorously high standards. "Writers thought because they wrote long speeches for me and had me talking fast and using a lot of non sequiturs and silly puns, that was all there was to it," he said. "That's my style all right. The trouble is, a lot of writers forgot to be funny along with it." That proved to be the case in *A Night in Casablanca,* whose gags, wrote a *New York Times* commentator, "sound as wheezy as an old Model T panting uphill on two cylinders."

Groucho, Chico, and Harpo once again went their
separate ways, never again to do a conventional Marx
Brothers film. The trio had worked together for 30 years.
Although Groucho had always been the team's kingpin,
each brother was equally responsible for its success.

The Marx Brothers reunited
in *A Night in Casablanca,*
which was released in 1946.

The Marx Brothers, from left to right, Gummo, Groucho, Harpo, Chico, and Zeppo, reunite at Groucho's home in Beverly Hills, circa 1938. After the act split up, Harpo and Chico never again achieved the popularity they had enjoyed in the 1930s and 1940s.

Each played off the other with panache to cook up the unique brew that continues today to tickle the funny bones of millions of devoted fans. "You couldn't direct the Marx Brothers any more than you could a Chaplin or a clown who had been doing the same number for many years," said Robert Florey, director of *The Cocoanuts.* "They did what they did and that was it."

Their synergy was remarkable, for Chico, Harpo, and Groucho were as dissimilar in temperament as if they had been born in separate countries, as their characters suggested. Of Chico and his chronically dissolute nature, Groucho once wrote, "Because he was my brother I loved him. Because he was selfish and irresponsible, I had little respect for him." Yet he also grudgingly admitted of his eldest brother that "the actor behind him brought the least preparation to his work, and it irritated me that he got away with it, which may prove that his was a more natural talent than mine." As for Harpo, his favorite brother, Groucho once said, "He inherited all my mother's good qualities—kindness, understanding, and friendliness. I got what was left."

After the Marx Brothers split up, Harpo and Chico never again achieved the fame they had enjoyed in the 1930s and early 1940s. But Groucho had a knack for reinventing himself when necessary, and he was about to become more celebrated than ever—in an entirely new medium.

7 ★ You Bet Your Life

N APRIL 1947, Groucho gave a radio performance that transformed his career. He had been invited to participate in a two-hour radio special hosted by Bob Hope, another renowned comedian. In the skit prepared for him, Groucho was to depict a traveling salesman paying a call on Hope, whose character ran a radio station in the middle of North Africa's Sahara Desert.

For several reasons, Groucho felt out of sorts that day. It had been 10 years since his last resounding film success, *A Day at the Races,* and unlike other comedians such as Jack Benny, Groucho had only halting success on radio. To rub it in, Groucho merely had a bit role in the two-hour special. So many stars preceded him on the program that by the time he came on, he had been forced to wait far longer than he had been warned. Groucho hated to be kept waiting.

So when Hope, following the script, said, "Why, Groucho Marx! What are you doing way out here in the Sahara Desert?" Groucho made a decision that inadvertently jump-started his idle career. Abandoning the script, he replied, "Desert, hell! I've been standing in a draughty corridor for 45

In August 1953, Groucho appears on NBC-TV's "You Bet Your Life." His quiz show, which had originated on radio in 1947, became so popular that the networks had a bidding war for the rights to the television version.

minutes." That line broke up both Hope and the studio audience. Buoyed by their reaction and in a feisty mood, Groucho began ad-libbing, and Hope, entering into the spirit of the moment, followed suit. Before the show's producers could decide how to stop them, recalled Arthur Marx, "the two comics had made an absolute shambles of their carefully prepared show." Although flabbergasted, the producers admitted, added Arthur Marx, "that in 20 years of radio they had never before heard such a hilarious performance."

Fortunately for Groucho, his improvised performance also reached the ears of a young producer named John Guedel, who happened to be sitting in the audience. Guedel, who marveled at Groucho's spontaneous creativity, approached him in his dressing room after the show. "Hiring you to do a show in which you read the script," he said, "is like buying a Cadillac to haul coal." Guedel offered to devise a radio show for Groucho that would allow him to ad-lib to his heart's content. Three days later, Guedel appeared with a draft format of the show, which would dominate the next 15 years of Groucho's life.

"You Bet Your Life" was a comedy program that masqueraded as a quiz show. As on most quiz shows today, contestants on "You Bet Your Life" won money by correctly answering questions that Groucho put to them. But like the plot in a Marx Brothers film, the question-and-answer format served only as scaffolding to support Groucho's waggishness. The quiz portion occupied about half of the program; during the remainder, Groucho interviewed his guests before a live studio audience, much as late-night TV hosts like David Letterman and Jay Leno do today. This was Groucho's chance to be funny, and it was the reason that, by 1955, his combined radio-television audience had reached an estimated 35 million Americans.

During the tête-à-tête with a contestant, Groucho drew upon an almost limitless source of ad-libbing techniques.

Groucho: You don't mind if I ask you a few personal questions, do you?
Model: If they're not too embarrassing.
Groucho: Don't give it another thought. I've asked thousands of questions on this show and I've yet to be embarrassed.
Groucho: What was your reaction to this American girl the first time you saw her?
Man: It was love at first sight. My heart was on fire.
Groucho: Your hat was on fire? Why didn't you take your hat off if you were wooing a girl?

Even when a contestant turned the tables and leveled a question at him, Groucho was prepared:

Bowler: Did you ever bowl yourself?
Groucho: Well, I didn't bowl myself, I used a ball. I tried it myself, but I never could get down the alley. I was always in the gutter. Even when I wasn't bowling.

"You Bet Your Life" broke new ground for Groucho. First, he updated his image. "He'd always been the raffish anti-Establishment destroyer," said Irving Brecher, who wrote the screenplays for *At the Circus* and *Go West*. "Now he was a more sedate man, dressed in a business suit with his hair neatly combed, holding a cigar, peering over his glasses, asking questions and making comments that were funny." And his mustache was his own; as he put it, "I bought it from the upstairs maid."

Second, for the first time in his career, Groucho dealt with everyday people, rather than with fictional characters dreamed up by jokesmiths. Each new profession, sport, or hobby that contestants revealed served as grist for Groucho's mill, such as the tree surgeon whom Groucho asked, "Have you ever fallen out of a patient?" Despite the insults that peppered every other phrase,

Groucho gives his daughter Melinda some pointers about playing pool. John Guedel had encouraged Groucho to open many of his "You Bet Your Life" episodes with some account about his daughter to show that he was a devoted family man.

Groucho's inherently warm personality came out. Previous sponsors had dropped him, Guedel thought, because listeners perceived him as cold and distant. Guedel encouraged him to open up by beginning many "You Bet Your Life" episodes with an anecdote about his daughter Mclinda. That immediately told the audience that, despite the barbs he flung at innocent contestants, Groucho was a kindhearted family man.

Contestants rarely took offense at Groucho's slights. In fact, as Howard Harris, one of the show's writers, said, "if they weren't insulted they were insulted." Often Groucho's digs were so absurd that no one *could* take offense, such as the housewife to whom Groucho said, "Your husband has a very good head for business, and if you take my advice you'll have it examined first thing in the morning."

Guedel's blueprint worked like a charm. A year after Groucho went on the air in October 1947, he won the most coveted radio broadcasting award, the Peabody, "for outstanding entertainment during 1948." The show's sponsor, the Elgin-American Watch Company, sold out its entire stock of merchandise in the two seasons it was associated with the program. Almost immediately, the three television networks began negotiating with Guedel for a TV version of "You Bet Your Life." At long last, Groucho's career was again off and running.

Groucho's good fortune, however, was tainted by disappointments. *Time for Elizabeth,* a light comedy he cowrote with playwright Norman Krasna, opened on Broadway in 1948. The pair wrote the lead role for Groucho, but he had to bow out because of other commitments, and the part went to actor Otto Kruger. The show closed after eight performances. "If only I could have been assured of that," Groucho remarked, "I should have been glad to take on the part myself."

Other commitments included starring in *Love Happy,* the last film in which the Marx Brothers appear together. Groucho played private detective Sam Grunion, but he only made cameo appearances. *Love Happy* was Harpo's pageant: he wrote it and played the lead. As always, Harpo plays "the *enfant terrible* who speaks eloquently the fluid, boundlessly fertile poetry of mime," wrote Paul

Zimmerman and Burt Goldblatt. The film's greatest claim to fame was that it introduced a young actress who would soon set the world afire. "For her one scene, she wore a dress cut so low that I couldn't remember the dialogue," Groucho wrote. "Very soon, other men throughout the world were suffering similar fevers, for the girl was Marilyn Monroe."

After United Artists released the film on March 5, 1950, Joe Phidona of the *New York Herald Tribune* wrote, "The Marx Brothers, in slightly amended form, are back in the cinema world and the event is an occasion for celebration." The event might have been, but the film itself, notwithstanding Harpo's mute wizardry, had little to distinguish it as a Marx Brothers picture. Groucho deemed *Love Happy* "a terrible picture, and I've tried to blot it out of my mind."

Groucho's second marriage steadily deteriorated throughout the late 1940s. Like his first wife, Ruth, Kay turned to drinking to find the solace she failed to get from the workaholic Groucho. In 1950 they divorced, with Groucho gaining custody of their four-year-old daughter, Melinda.

As he had done two decades earlier, after he lost both his mother and his life savings within a single year, Groucho rose like a phoenix from the ashes of his personal life to reach a higher level of notoriety than he had ever known. In 1949, NBC won the bidding war for a television version of "You Bet Your Life." Groucho once had disparaged what he dubbed the one-eyed monster: "I must say I find television very educational. The minute somebody turns it on, I go into the library and read a good book." Yet he was never one to refuse a hot opportunity, so in the fall of 1950 he began his first TV appearances. Because arguably half of Groucho's legendary delivery was visual, the TV version became an instant triumph. Within six months, the Academy of

Television Arts and Sciences named Groucho the Outstanding Television Personality of 1950. Two years later, he made the cover of *Time* magazine for the second time—in this case without his brothers.

The normally hypersensitive Groucho was so popular that even his few detractors dealt only glancing blows. He could afford to laugh at Phyllis McGinley's couplet in the *New Yorker:* "I'd rather sleep in public parks / Than be on the show with Groucho Marx." And when an unscrupulous magazine called *Confidential* published an article panning him and his quiz show, which it claimed was rigged, Groucho did not sue for libel, as many people do today at the least provocation. He simply sent a letter

Groucho is photographed in 1958 with his third wife, Eden (left), and his daughter Miriam, before his appearance in the play, *Time for Elizabeth,* which he cowrote with Norman Krasna 10 years earlier.

to the editor that is considered one of his wittiest re-
torts: "Gentlemen, if you continue to publish slanderous
pieces about me, I shall feel compelled to cancel my
subscription."

Groucho had reached the zenith of his comic powers.
Time maintained that his matchless delivery was "as good
or better than ever: the perfectly timed twitch of the
brows; the play of the luminous brown eyes—now rolling
with naughty thoughts, now staring through the spectacles with only half-amused contempt; the acidulous,
faint smile; the touch of fuming disgust in the voice
('That's as shifty an answer as I ever heard'); above all,
the effrontery."

Groucho's new currency owed much to the tenor of
the times. President Dwight D. Eisenhower's election in
1952 ushered in a material prosperity unequaled in memory, providing the foundation for the nation's growth
into an economic and military superpower. Yet the exu-
berance many Americans felt was tempered by dread—a
dread of Communism, which brought on the war in
Korea in 1950 and the rise of a rival superpower, the
Soviet Union; and a more insidious dread of nuclear war
that, beginning in the early 1950s, had citizens rushing
to build atomic bomb shelters. As an antidote, Americans
threw themselves into such inane fads as hula hoops,
ducktail haircuts, and telephone-booth stuffing. Television, too, supplied reassurance through feel-good shows
like "Leave It to Beaver" and "Father Knows Best"—and
enabled people to laugh themselves silly watching such
sidesplitters as "I Love Lucy," "The Honeymooners," and
"You Bet Your Life."

Americans also sought security in the family, and in
this, Groucho also kept up with the Joneses. In 1954, at
age 64, he married a 21-year-old actress named Eden
Hartford in Sun Valley, Idaho. He built his new wife a
$300,000 home in the upscale Trousdale section of Bev-

Groucho unfurls his
autobiography, *Groucho
and Me,* in 1959.

erly Hills, and he also purchased a bungalow in Palm
Springs, the city where his four brothers lived.

As Groucho's fame waxed on television, it waned in
the movies. In 1947, he played opposite Brazilian actress
Carmen Miranda in *Copacabana,* a romantic comedy
about an agent who creates two acts out of one client,
which proves awkward when both acts are needed at the
same time. *Copacabana* was the first film in which

Groucho appeared without his brothers. "They must have known something I didn't," he said in dismissing the movie, which received tepid reviews. He went on in the 1950s to accept supporting roles in five more pictures: *Mr. Music,* starring Bing Crosby (1950); *Double Dynamite,* with Jane Russell and Frank Sinatra (1951); *A Girl in Every Port,* featuring William Bendix and Marie Wilson (1951); *Will Success Spoil Rock Hunter?,* starring Jayne Mansfield and Tony Randall (1957); and *The Story of Mankind* (1957). *The Story of Mankind* featured Chico, Harpo, and Groucho—though in different segments—as well as a host of other stars in what *Newsweek* called "a poor excuse to use a batch of available actors in some of the weirdest casting ever committed." As Groucho's roles in each of these five films demonstrate, casting a Marx brother in anything but a Marx Brothers movie was regrettable.

Groucho plays Ko-Ko the Lord High Executioner in Gilbert and Sullivan's operetta *The Mikado,* which was televised on the "Bell Telephone Hour" in April 1960. Groucho had long aspired to act in the operetta, his favorite.

As the 1950s drew to a close, "You Bet Your Life" began a gradual slide in popularity. Times were changing, and Groucho's *shtick* (routine) began to appear dated. Realizing the show's hours were numbered, Groucho engaged in other work. In 1959 he published his autobiography, *Groucho and Me,* which became a *New York Times* bestseller for several weeks. The same year, he appeared with his brothers for the last time in a General Electric Theater television special called *The Incredible Jewel Robbery.* And in April 1960 he realized a dream by playing Ko-Ko the Lord High Executioner in a TV production of *The Mikado,* an operetta by his favorite playwright-composer team, Gilbert and Sullivan. *Time* had reported in its 1952 cover story that one of Groucho's favorite occupations was "sitting for long hours in his den strumming Gilbert and Sullivan (at which he is an expert) on his guitar."

The following year, 1961, was a year of endings for Groucho. "You Bet Your Life" went off the air after 11 seasons on NBC, which had made it the most popular TV quiz show of all time. Groucho's best friend, Norman Krasna, moved to Switzerland. And the man he most respected, George Kaufman, died. Groucho once confided to Arthur that if there was an afterlife, he would like to spend it with Abraham Lincoln, William Shakespeare, and George Kaufman.

The biggest blow came in October 1961, when Chico died of a heart attack. An editorial in the *New York Times* the day after his death lamented, "While Groucho, Harpo, and Chico were all available, there was always an outside chance that they might vandalize the land of cuckoo once more. It can never be. The funniest team of 20th century mountebanks is broken beyond repair. Alas, poor Chico. Alas, ourselves." On the way back from the funeral, Arthur remembered, Groucho and Harpo cut down their brother, but that night, Groucho, who was normally a teetotaler, drank four whiskeys in a row. "I guess he felt worse about losing Chico than he let on," Arthur wrote.

Symbolically, Chico's passing marked an effective end to Groucho's career. Groucho was then 71 years old and had been in show business for well over half a century. Yet, though he could afford to live out the rest of his days quietly, Groucho had other ideas.

8 The Last Laugh

THE 1960s REPRESENTED a time of uncertainty for Groucho, as they did for the country. America was slipping into the deadliest, least-understood war in its history, in Vietnam, while trying to come to terms with increasingly complex civil rights issues and a rebellious younger generation. For Groucho, the decade brought fewer career opportunities and deteriorating personal health and family relations. As he had done in the past, he would work through his troubles to achieve new glory, but his seventies were the most dispirited years of his life.

Although Chico's death in 1961 saddened him, an even more grievous blow came in 1964 when Harpo, Groucho's favorite brother, died following open-heart surgery. M-G-M head Samuel Goldwyn spoke for everyone who knew Harpo when he said he was "one of the gentlest human beings I have ever known." Groucho, whom Arthur found more broken up than he had ever seen him, wrote to his friend Betty Comden, "Having worked with Harpo for 40 years . . . his death left quite a void in my life. He was worth all the wonderful adjectives that were used to describe him. He was a nice

Groucho poses with his son, Arthur. Arthur later wrote a book about his father, entitled *My Life with Groucho: A Son's Eye View.*

man in the fullest sense of the word. He loved life and lived it joyously and deeply, and that's about as good an epitaph as anyone can have."

Though his brothers' deaths reminded him of his own advancing years, Groucho was not the retiring type. To him, retirement would have meant admitting he was "washed up." So after "You Bet Your Life" ended, he tried his best to stay in show business. Unfortunately, his efforts met with only measured success. In 1962 he began broadcasting another quiz-cum-talk show dreamed up by John Guedel, "Tell It to Groucho," in which Groucho responded to audience members' questions about current events. CBS canceled the show after 20 episodes because of poor ratings. In the mid-1960s he briefly hosted two programs, "The Hollywood Palace" and "The Tonight Show," and he made sporadic guest appearances on other stars' talk shows, including "The Dick Cavett Show." In 1965 he went before live studio audiences in London to do an English version of "You Bet Your Life," but his quirky, dyed-in-the-wool American humor missed its mark, and the show was discontinued after 13 weeks. A final dud came in 1968, when Groucho accepted the role of "God," the head of a crime syndicate, in Otto Preminger's film *Skidoo.* "Both the picture and my role were God-awful," Groucho said.

He published two books in the 1960s, but both were passive efforts featuring work he had written in better times. The first, *Memoirs of a Mangy Lover,* a collection of his best magazine pieces, came out in 1964. In an article entitled "On (and off) Bodies," Groucho writes:

> The neck is a short drain pipe that rises up out of the shoulders and disappears into the bottom of the head. It is usually decorated with an Adam's apple and an untidy collar. The Adam's apple is a medium-sized meat ball that keeps running up and down the front of the neck looking helplessly for its mate. It is an unfortunate monstrosity that

nature, angry at her handiwork, has left on our doorstep, and there is nothing we can do about it. Many people attempt to hide it by wrapping a necktie around it, but in most cases the necktie is even uglier than the apple.

The other book, published in 1967, was *The Groucho Letters: Letters from and to Groucho Marx.* The book enshrines correspondence from the 1940s on, with family, friends, and famous people. (Groucho corresponded regularly with the poet T. S. Eliot, the novelist Sidney Sheldon, and the writer E. B. White.) As ever, his brief notes to people he did not know often brought out his most characteristic lines. In 1951 he had written to the president of Elgin-American Watch Company, the first sponsor of "You Bet Your Life," thanking him for the gift of a gold watch. "The watch is a thing of beauty and will be a joy forever," Groucho wrote, "and I would have thanked you sooner, but I purposely waited a week, for I wanted to be sure that the lousy thing would run."

In 1968, Groucho (right) played "God" in Otto Preminger's *Skidoo*. The movie was a bomb at the box office, which led Groucho to say, "Both the picture and my role were God-awful."

Health problems exacerbated his efforts to keep his career afloat. By 1970, when he made a surprise appearance onstage after the premiere of *Minnie's Boys,* a musical about the rise of the Marx Brothers, he looked, according to Arthur, "old, frail, and ill." Groucho had rarely been sick, complaining now and then only of a mysterious "grippy feeling." But in the 1960s he developed a severe bladder problem and suffered several minor strokes that brought him, Arthur declared, "to the brink of senility."

Troubled by his ill health and nostalgic for his glory days, Groucho became cranky and careless. During

President Richard Nixon's first term in office (1969–72), Groucho let slip, during an interview with the left-wing newspaper the *Berkeley Barb,* that the only hope for the country was Nixon's assassination. Because it is a federal offense to even indirectly threaten the president's life, the Federal Bureau of Investigation put the nearly octogenarian Groucho under surveillance and actually listed him as a threat to the president. About the same time, producer Arthur Whitelaw, in a token gesture, named Groucho production consultant on *Minnie's Boys.* This was a time—mid-1969—when the sickly Groucho "was in no shape to be consulted about anything," recalled Arthur Marx. When casting for the musical began, Groucho adamantly refused to let the Jewish comedian Totie Fields play the role of his mother, Minnie. When asked why, he said simply, "the world thinks we're Italian." Even though most people involved in the production agreed Fields was perfect for the role, Whitelaw finally gave in to Groucho's wishes and awarded the part to actress Shelley Winters, who fit Groucho's image of his blond, Germanic-looking mother. (*Minnie's Boys* closed after 60 regular performances with a loss of $500,000.)

Groucho's stubbornness about the image he wanted portrayed of his mother brought out an enigmatic side of his character—namely, what he thought of being Jewish. He never married a Jewish woman, was never married by a rabbi, and never took his children to temple, claiming, reported his son, that all "organized religion is hogwash." Groucho once explained away this lifelong disregard for his ethnicity. "We Marx Brothers never denied our Jewishness. We simply didn't use it. We could have safely fallen back on the Yiddish theater, making secure careers for ourselves. But our act was designed from the start to have a broad appeal." Arthur Marx believes his father's denial stemmed from growing up in a tough New York neighborhood in which the dominant group, the Irish, always beat up on the Jewish kids. In the end, as with everything, Groucho chose to make light of the issue. When a swim club denied him membership because he was Jewish, he asked, "Can my son go in up to his knees? He's only half-Jewish."

As Groucho's health deteriorated, so did his family life. In 1968 he threw a lavish party to celebrate the marriage of his daughter Melinda, yet two weeks later, she ran off with another man. The same year, his wife Eden walked out on him after 14 years of marriage; they were divorced in 1969. Groucho, who cherished family ties, became a recluse, living alone in the spacious Beverly Hills home he had built for Eden a decade earlier. His sole companions were his housekeeper, Martha Brooks, and a white poodle, Elsie, which Arthur had given him. When Elsie was killed by a car, Groucho told Arthur he felt more downcast than when Harpo and Chico had died, a sign of how lonely and depressed Groucho had become.

Then, in August 1971, what Groucho deemed a miracle occurred. A young woman named Erin Fleming answered an ad Groucho had placed for a secretary. For an ailing and downtrodden Groucho she was a godsend. She revived him—and his sputtering career.

The previous fall he had had a successful bladder operation, and although he had suffered another stroke

Shelley Winters plays Minnie Marx in the 1970 musical *Minnie's Boys* at New York's Imperial Theatre. Producer Arthur Whitelaw asked Groucho to serve as consultant on the production, which eventually lost about $500,000.

Groucho and his companion Erin Fleming attend the opening of *Gypsy* on Broadway. Groucho, who had become somewhat reclusive and had problems with his health, believed Erin was a godsend when he hired her in 1971.

in 1971, his mind was still spry enough to leave a live audience in stitches. Groucho got his chance to do just that in 1972, when he was invited to perform a solo show at Carnegie Hall in New York, one of the world's premier performance centers. Tickets were sold out for weeks in advance, because it was clear this would be the 81-year-old Groucho's swan song on the stage. Accompanied on piano by the composer Marvin Hamlisch, Groucho gave a dry run of his act before a crowd at Iowa State University, then traveled to New York for the May 6 performance.

"I hadn't performed in New York since 1930 [in *Animal Crackers*] and the press turned out en masse to find out why I chose to come back," he wrote. "I said it had taken that much time for New York to forget about my last performance there." These and other jokes, songs, and routines that he pulled from his still-serviceable memory broke up the Carnegie Hall audience, much of which dressed as Captain Spaulding and other Groucho characters—and all of which honored him at the end with a sustained standing ovation. The *New York Times* lauded Groucho the next day, and A & M Records later released a double-record album commemorating the show.

Groucho's triumph at Carnegie Hall spawned a series of distinguished commendations. Two months after his New York performance, Groucho flew to France to receive the French government's Legion of Honor. Only two other foreigners, director Alfred Hitchcock and actor-director Charlie Chaplin, had previously received this prestigious award, which entertainers coveted as much as an Academy Award. When Cannes Film Festival president Robert Favre Le Bret presented him with the medal, Groucho, true to form, declared, "All the way from Beverly Hills for this! It's not even real gold." Only Groucho Marx could get away with such "unsquelchable effrontery," and Le Bret, rather than take offense, merely laughed.

Not to be upstaged, the Academy Awards followed suit two years later. On April 2, 1974, at the Los Angeles Music Center, actor Jack Lemmon presented Groucho with a special Oscar for his "brilliant creativity and for the unequaled achievements of the Marx Brothers in the art of motion picture comedy." In his remarks, an emotional Groucho thanked Margaret Dumont, Erin Fleming, and his mother, Minnie, "without whom we would have been a failure," and added that he only wished Harpo and Chico could be standing there with him.

The tributes kept coming. When Groucho turned 85 on October 2, 1975, Los Angeles mayor Tom Bradley proclaimed the day Groucho Marx Day. The following year, Groucho won the Sunair Humanitarian Award, and the publisher Bobbs-Merrill reissued a commemorative edition of his first book, *Beds*. The occasional speeches that Fleming arranged for him to give at colleges and universities became so popular that a 1975 poll showed that after the diplomat Henry Kissinger, Groucho was the most sought-after lecturer in America. Another poll that year, of incoming college freshmen, revealed that after Jesus Christ and the humanitarian Albert Schweitzer, Groucho Marx was the man they most admired.

Perhaps the most gratifying recognition Groucho received was the nationwide resurgence in the popularity of Marx Brothers films. In 1973, *Animal Crackers,* which had not been seen publicly for almost 20 years because of contractual disputes, was shown in New York. When Groucho arrived at the showing, he was mobbed by a surging crowd of fans, who had to be held back by

On April 2, 1974, Groucho holds the honorary Oscar awarded to him by the Motion Picture Academy for his "brilliant creativity and for the unequalled achievements of the Marx Brothers in the art of motion picture comedy."

policemen on horseback. "One of the horses asked me for my autograph," Groucho remarked. "All I gave him was a hoarse laugh." And more than 40 years after its poor initial release, *Duck Soup,* whose antiwar, antiestablishment tone struck a chord with disillusioned Vietnam-era youth, finally enjoyed the popularity it deserved.

These accolades came none too soon. In early 1977, while attending a birthday party for the comedian George Burns, Groucho collapsed. He had had a small heart attack. In the coming months, his health deteriorated rapidly. When Gummo died on April 21, Groucho was not told of his death for fear it would upset him too much. Though not in full use of his faculties, Groucho was already caught up in a vicious family battle, principally between his son, Arthur, and his secretary, Erin Fleming. Ever since she had arrived on the scene six years earlier, Arthur charged, she had coerced the increasingly senile Groucho into buying her a house, getting her bit parts in movies, making her the conservator of his estate, and even trying to get him to adopt her. (In the end, Bank of America, the executor of Groucho's estate, brought suit against Erin Fleming seeking recovery of funds and properties she had obtained over those six years; the bank won its case, but it was not until 1988 that Groucho's estate—largely diminished from court costs and attorneys' fees—was disbursed to family members.)

The strife between his beloved son and his nurselike secretary—not to mention just plain old age—took their toll on the 86-year-old Groucho. On August 19, at 7:25 in the evening, he died of pneumonia at Cedars Sinai Medical Center in Los Angeles. "I had been apprehensive about watching him or anyone else die," wrote Arthur Marx, who was at his father's side in the final minutes. "But I had nothing to fear. It was as if peace had finally descended upon my troubled father. He looked completely at rest."

Groucho relaxes at home on January 18, 1977, seven months before his death. After Groucho died, comedian and filmmaker Woody Allen said, "Groucho Marx was the best comedian this country ever produced."

Groucho Marx had worked in show business for almost seven decades, mastering five different media: theater, film, radio, television, and the lecture hall. The collected papers of this seventh-grade dropout now reside in the Library of Congress, and the Smithsonian Institution acquired his photograph collection. Many consider him the greatest comedian of the century, who influenced—and continues to influence—whole generations of comics. In 1974, comedian-actor Bill Cosby asked Groucho to appear on his television program "The Bill Cosby Show" as his guest. Twenty years later, Cosby, commenting on Groucho's guest appearance said,

> Groucho and I ad-libbed a lot. I feel ad-libbing is relying on everything that you can think of in order to come up with humor, on your feet, not knowing when or where. . . . Groucho thought funny, and ad-libbing is thinking funny. It doesn't make any difference whether you've had

this particular line and you've used it before. When and if the line comes, you don't know when it's coming, and then you use it, you are ad-libbing. You have to be on top of it. You have to play the moment. And that's what Groucho was absolutely brilliant with.

In fact, Cosby appreciated Groucho and "You Bet Your Life" so much that in 1993 he got the chance to produce and perform his own version of the show on NBC.

Another of Groucho's disciples is the comedian and filmmaker Woody Allen, who wrote what could serve as the finest epitaph to Groucho's life:

Some years back, after a childhood of preoccupation with comedy that led to observing the styles of all the great comedians, I came to the conclusion that Groucho Marx was the best comedian this country ever produced. Now I am more convinced than ever that I was right. I can't think of a comedian who combined a totally original physical conception that was hilarious with a matchless verbal delivery. I believe there is a natural inborn greatness in Groucho that defies close analysis as it does with any genuine artist. He is simply unique in the same way that Picasso or Stravinsky are, and I believe his outrageous unsentimental disregard for order will be equally as funny a thousand years from now. In addition to this, he makes me laugh.

Groucho, fittingly, had the last laugh. Several times he had implored Arthur not to bury him—an act he considered barbaric—but rather to cremate his body and do whatever seemed appropriate with the ashes. Arthur acceded to his father's wishes and, following a small family gathering at Arthur's house, had his ashes interred in a vault in a San Fernando Valley cemetery. A few days later, while going through Groucho's effects, Arthur found a letter from his father to him. In it, Groucho said he had changed his mind. He wanted to be buried alongside the body of Marilyn Monroe.

Further Reading ★ ★ ★ ★ ★ ★ ★ ★ ★ ★ ★ ★ ★

Anobile, Richard J., ed. *Why a Duck? Visual and Verbal Gems from the Marx Brothers Movies.* New York: Darien House, 1971.

Arce, Hector. *Groucho.* New York: Putnam, 1979.

Chandler, Charlotte. *Hello, I Must Be Going: Groucho and His Friends.* Garden City, NY: Doubleday, 1978; Secaucus, NJ: Citadel Press, 1992.

Crichton, Kyle Samuel. *The Marx Brothers.* Garden City, NY: Doubleday, 1950.

Eyles, Allen. *The Marx Brothers: Their World of Comedy.* New York: Barnes, 1974.

Marx, Arthur. *My Life with Groucho: A Son's Eye View.* London: Robson Books, 1988.

Marx, Groucho. *Groucho and Me.* New York: Geis, 1959.

———. *The Groucho Letters: Letters from and to Groucho Marx.* New York: Simon & Schuster, 1967.

———. *The GrouchoPhile: An Illustrated Life.* Indianapolis: Bobbs-Merrill, 1976.

———. *Love, Groucho: Letters from Groucho Marx to His Daughter Miriam.* Boston: Faber & Faber, 1992.

———. *Memoirs of a Mangy Lover.* New York: Geis, 1963.

———. *The Secret Word Is Groucho.* New York: Putnam, 1976.

Marx, Groucho, and Richard J. Anobile. *The Marx Bros. Scrapbook.* New York: Darien House, 1973.

Marx, Harpo, and Rowland Barber. *Harpo Speaks!* 1961. Reprint. New York: Proscenium Publishers, 1985.

Marx, Maxine. *Growing Up with Chico.* Englewood Cliffs, NJ: Prentice-Hall, 1980.

Wolf, William. *The Marx Brothers.* New York: Pyramid Communications, 1975.

Zimmerman, Paul D., and Burt Goldblatt. *The Marx Brothers at the Movies.* New York: Putnam, 1968.

Chronology ★ ★ ★ ★ ★ ★ ★ ★ ★ ★ ★ ★ ★ ★ ★ ★

1890	Born Julius Henry Marx on October 2 in New York City
1907	Joins the Four Nightingales
1910	Writes *Fun in Hi Skule*
1914	Begins performing *Home Again*
1920	Marries Ruth Johnson; makes silent film *Humor Risk*
1921	Ruth and Groucho's son, Arthur, is born
1924	*I'll Say She Is* opens on Broadway
1925	*The Cocoanuts* opens on Broadway
1927	Ruth and Groucho's daughter, Miriam, is born
1928	*Animal Crackers* opens on Broadway
1929	The film *The Cocoanuts* is released; mother, Minnie Marx, dies
1930	The film *Animal Crackers* is released; Groucho publishes first book, *Beds*
1932	On August 13, the Marx Brothers appear on the cover of *Time* magazine; film *Horse Feathers* is released
1933	Groucho and Chico perform radio show "Flywheel, Shyster, and Flywheel"; film *Duck Soup* is released
1934	Plays first straight role in summer theater in Skowhegan, Maine
1935	Movie *A Night at the Opera* is released
1936	Irving Thalberg dies; Simon "Frenchie" Marx dies
1937	*A Day at the Races* is released
1938	*Room Service* is released
1939	*At the Circus* is released
1940	*Go West* is released

1941	*The Big Store* is released; Groucho publishes second book, *Many Happy Returns*
1942	Marx Brothers disband after 30 years in show business; Groucho divorces Ruth; tours country for war effort
1945	Marries Kay Gorcey
1946	Daughter Melinda is born; *A Night in Casablanca* is released
1947	"You Bet Your Life" is broadcast on radio
1948	Groucho wins radio's prestigious Peabody award
1950	*Love Happy* is released; Groucho divorces Kay; "You Bet Your Life" is televised; Groucho is named Outstanding Television Personality of the Year
1952	Appears on the cover of the December 31 issue of *Time*
1954	Marries Eden Hartford
1959	Publishes third book, *Groucho and Me*
1961	Chico dies; "You Bet Your Life" ends after 11 seasons
1964	Harpo dies; Groucho publishes fourth book, *Memoirs of a Mangy Lover*
1967	Publishes fifth book, *The Groucho Letters*
1969	Divorces Eden
1972	On May 6, appears at New York's Carnegie Hall; receives French Legion of Honor at Cannes Film Festival
1974	Receives honorary Academy Award
1975	In honor of Groucho's 85th birthday, the mayor of Los Angeles proclaims October 2 Groucho Marx Day
1977	Groucho Marx dies on August 19 in Los Angeles, California, at the age of 86

Index ★

Peter Tyson, who regrets never having been personally insulted by Groucho, is a science journalist and managing editor of *Earthwatch* magazine in Boston, Massachusetts. A semiprofessional photographer, he has traveled to many remote regions, including Antarctica, Greenland, Baffin Island, Tibet, Siberia, Sumatra, Madagascar, and the North Slope of Alaska. He pores over Marx Brothers videos in Arlington, Massachusetts, with his wife and stepson.

Leeza Gibbons is a reporter for and cohost of the nationally syndicated television program "Entertainment Tonight" and NBC's daily talk show "Leeza." A graduate of the University of South Carolina's School of Journalism, Gibbons joined the on-air staff of "Entertainment Tonight" in 1984 after cohosting WCBS-TV's "Two on the Town" in New York City. Prior to that, she cohosted "PM Magazine" on WFAA-TV in Dallas, Texas, and on KFDM-TV in Beaumont, Texas. Gibbons also hosts the annual "Miss Universe," "Miss U.S.A.," and "Miss Teen U.S.A." pageants, as well as the annual Hollywood Christmas Parade. She is active in a number of charities and has served as the national chairperson for the Spinal Muscular Atrophy Division of the Muscular Dystrophy Association; each September, Gibbons cohosts the National MDA Telethon with Jerry Lewis.